ONE
Lonely
THANKSGIVING

ONE
Lonely
THANKSGIVING
a novella

SANDY FAYE MAUCK

One Lonely Thanksgiving

*Book 1 **Cherished Thanksgivings***

Christian Historical Romance

Copyright © 2016 Sandy Faye Mauck

Lightkeepers Press

1970 N. Leslie St. Ste. 524

Pahrump, NV 89060

ISBN: 978-09968806-4-0 (pbk)

ISBN: 978-09968806-3-3 (e-book)

Cover Design: <u>Roseanna White Book Covers</u>

Dedication

This book is dedicated to all those
who have suffered loneliness, and those
who have been left alone by loss of family,
young and old. God cares far more than we
know and He orchestrates and entwines
people into our lives to bring joy,
hope and new life.

A special dedication to my daughter-in-law,
Kelly,
who lost her young brother and her parents and
knows too well that pang of loss.

And as always my books are dedicated
to my Savior, for without Him, life has no
meaning and books no reason for being.

God setteth
the solitary
in families.

Psalm 68:6

Chapter 1

Thanksgiving 1905

It was the day before Thanksgiving and they left without her—again.

Margie stood outside the gate, glaring face-to-face with the stately Queen Anne, looming in all its glory. Brilliantly colored birch and maples framed the impressive house. Such a lovely home yet without the slightest trace of comfort to her lonely soul.

But feeling alone wasn't the only thing bothering her. She sensed something was about to change. Her gaze jumped from the cupola on the house up to the sky. Snow clouds! A chilly northern gust whipped through the opening in her coat, nudging her through the gate and up the steps. She peered toward the side of the house as she went. There was a decided lack of activity, no gardener nor servants. Was her family really so heartless to leave her completely alone on a holiday?

She opened the door into the normally bustling house, now void of people. Like apparitions she saw a vision of her spoiled cousins like they might have acted as they prepared to leave earlier that day. Geri, telling them they are all babies while Ralston dusted his top hat. Lala donning her expensive fur collar, eager to show it to her frivolous friends. All the while the three older siblings attempting to ignore Nettie's incessant whining about being conveyed to some strange place she didn't want to go.

Margie shut off the imaginary playacting, rested against the closed door, and sighed. They were the only family she had, but they treated her as if she were an intruder. This time they left her no servants. Not a soul to talk to. She would never be so callous. Uncle Thornton and Aunt Millicent had probably left before their children and discharged the servants to leave after cleaning up after them. They probably planned it that way so they didn't have to deal with their ill-mannered, but "oh so perfect" nearly grown children.

The house seemed bereft of warmth in any way. The chill that permeated the inside was as icy as the way the family treated her since the day she arrived in the late spring. She tried to be pleasant to all of them but it didn't seem to make any difference.

Well, they weren't here —she should be glad.

She reluctantly pulled her coat off, hanging it near her hat and muffler on the deserted coat rack. She patted down the sleeve of her trusty coat. It had seen better days but then so had she. She'd also seen much better Thanksgivings. What would come of her life? Her head drooped and tears clung, veiling her vision.

Margie shivered, then went quickly to build a fire, trying to be brave, but her tears kept falling like fat raindrops on the logs as she placed them atop the kindling. When the fire roared to life, she rubbed her icy hands together, staring into the dancing flames.

She pulled her attention away from the fire. The parlor held many extravagant furnishings—some lovely, some hideous. She loved the hand-carved arches that led from room to room. But it was people that made a home. This could never be home for her. But why think of that now? What good can come of such thoughts? Mother and Father were gone to heaven. Jeff and his wife Adele were overseas, and Margie had buried Pepper, her beloved collie, before coming here to stay. She must face the fact that she was alone, even in her own uncle's house.

YOU ARE NOT ALONE.

Oh, Lord, I am sorry. I know you are here with me. Forgive me. Here I am acting as spoiled as my cousins, while Jeff works so hard on the mission field.

3

She stopped to pray for Jeff and Adele as she did so often throughout the day. If he were here, he would tell her, "Be brave little Pocahontas. God has a plan for your life." How she missed their fun times, Bible discussions, and prayer times. She wondered if she should go to Jeff in the Philippines. She shook her head.

No, I know that is not what you have for me, Lord. You do have a plan.

Hunger gnawed at her so she made her way to the kitchen. She was elated to see that the servants had at least cleaned everything before they left. Last time, it had all been left to her, even with some of the servants present. The house felt so enormous with only herself to entertain. However, she had to admit that it was a pleasant sort of silence, not having to listen to this family that lived so contentiously together.

Margie made herself a sandwich, with hot tea and a leftover pastry that Dahlia—her only friend—the household maid—had left her in the hidden place, as she often did. She went back to the parlor. Lured to the window, she sat on the window seat watching as the trees dropped their multicolored leaves. They were like drops of paint, coloring the snow for only a moment before being tucked away under the heavy white blanket that started to thicken.

The falling leaves ushered her back in time. Margie was ten years old, running for the pile of leaves that Jeff had just raked into an inviting mountain. He chastised her and then jumped in the pile with her. They threw up the leaves, giggling together. Pepper bounded from his lookout on the porch and jumped in barking. Father came out and stood with his arms crossed but he gave up on any reprimand and laughed, too.

Big fat snowflakes startled her out of her memories. The fascinating scene made her smile but she soon realized she must go get wood. The snow was accumulating quickly.

With the wood gathered, the fire blazing, Margie snuggled down into the chair to watch the snowfall and soon fell asleep.

She was dreaming of Pepper playing and barking when she realized it wasn't a dream. A dog was on the porch looking in the window, barking urgently. The collie had a gorgeous blue-black coat like Pepper, but it was partially covered in snow. It looked like a female by the shape of the nose. Was she hungry? Margie took a piece of her sandwich and opened the door. The collie nuzzled her leg but then backed up and barked, refusing her treat. Snow went flying off her back as she continued to bark. The dog then ran down the steps, turned in circles and barked again. Margie knew precisely what she wanted. The dog wanted Margie to follow. The tone of her bark was poignantly familiar.

"What is it, girl?"

The collie spun again and barked a bit more high-pitched, so Margie readied herself to go out into the storm.

She wondered what the disturbed collie had to show her, as she followed the dog out into the piling mass of white. The dog jumped the fence and waited for her. After making her way out the gate, that required some kicking and pulling, she followed the anxious dog toward a grove of elm trees. A car was parked next to the trees, slowly being covered by the thick snowflakes. Margie was apprehensive but the collie wouldn't let up. She kept whining and nosing at the door.

"All right, girl, I'm coming." She tried to hurry, but it was getting harder to see. When she arrived at the car where the collie had led her, she cautiously peered through the broken window.

Oh, Father, please let them be okay.

A man was hunched over the steering wheel, far too still. Her heart sank. She didn't see anyone else.

"Hello, sir? Are you all right?" she said, opening the door.

Was he dead? The thought made her freeze in place. She'd seen too much death. She didn't want to believe it.

Perhaps he was only drunk and passed out. Could he be one of her cousin Ralston's drinking buddies?

She fought with herself. She did not want to take care of some dangerous drunk! But he might not be and perhaps he had loved ones wondering after him. She felt for a pulse and was happy to feel that it pounded strongly.

He's alive, but now what? She couldn't drag him to the house by herself. Oh, why didn't Uncle Thornton leave at least one servant behind?

She was coated in snow. She had to think. The collie jumped up to lick her master's face and nuzzle his neck, but it didn't wake him.

Father, I need help. Give me wisdom. I feel completely helpless.

Instantly, the memory of Pepper pulling her around as a child sent her back toward the side of the house in a run. She went straight for the garage, found a sled and dragged it to the car.

With much exhausting maneuvering, she slowly brought the man out of the seat and down onto the sled, trying with all her strength to cradle his head.

"Umph, your master is heavy, girl." How would she get him into the house?

Well, we got this far, I guess you will make a way, Lord.

She pulled her muffler off and laid it on his face. Once she hooked the faithful collie to the sled rope, the dog seemed to know just what to do. The unlikely rescuers slowly coursed their way around to the side of the house, the collie pulling and Margie pushing, neither of them having an easy time of it. Margie kept him on the sled which was difficult as his long legs kept dragging off the back of the sled into the snow.

They managed to get the strange litter into the middle of the kitchen from the side door. She hoped they could get him closer to the fire but this would have to do. The rugs were too heavy to get over. At least he wouldn't freeze. But what was she to do with him now?

Chapter 2

Margie ran upstairs and gathered blankets to make a bed next to the sled. She made it up, then carefully slid him down onto it.

"Okay, girl, you keep him warm while I make a better fire in the stove."

The dog seemed to understand but as she started to curl up near her master, Margie called to her. "Wait, girl. Come here." She grabbed some toweling and dried the collie off as much as she could. "Okay, now you can go take care of him."

The faithful dog curled up near her master, resting her head on his arm. Her tiny brown eyebrows twitched back and forth watching Margie's every move. She could see the distress in the dog's eyes.

Once the stove was burning, Margie knelt down to see her patient. He seemed a kind-looking man, and well-dressed. However, he had scratches and some bruising starting to color his face. She cleaned off the scrapes praying as she did. She thought him to be a few years older than herself. Perhaps there would be something in his coat pocket that would identify him. Margie felt sheepish as she searched the stranger's pockets. She found a well-worn card like a valentine, with a sweet baby on it. In faded writing it said, "To Johnny, Don't forget your beloved Amy."

Margie's heart stirred at such a sweet sentiment. She looked down at his face. How lovely it would be to be someone's beloved. But she ignored any more thoughts about herself and decided to see how wet his feet were.

"Johnny, it is. Okay, Johnny, let's see if I can remove your shoes and get you some warm socks."

She found a pair of wool socks in Ralston's bureau and put them on the dormant man's feet. Now she would try to get help.

Margie went to the telephone and clicked for the operator. "Hello, hello…are you there?"

"Hello?" a distant voice said. "The weather—"

"Yes. We need a doctor at the Thornton residence on Maple Hill. There has been an accident. Hello, hello?"

The line went dead. She hoped the operator had heard her but she doubted it.

Please send a doctor, Father, I am not a nurse, I don't know what to do to help him.

Margie went back to the kitchen. The stove was heating nicely, but being on the floor was still too drafty.

She sat down next to him, patted the collie's head, and prayed for Johnny.

Oh, Father, I pray for this man's life and for his family that they won't be worried about him. And I know this sounds selfish, but I don't think I can stand to see another person die and this man is someone's beloved.

She looked at his peaceful, sleeping face. She hadn't had time to notice how handsome he was. Gently pushing back the wayward hair on his forehead, the palm of her hand fell down his soft cheek and the edge of his whiskers.

Big brown eyes batted at her. She snapped her hand back. Had he felt her hand touching his face? He began to look around.

"Don't be afraid. You've been in an accident."

"Snow," he said. "I hit something." He winced.

"Yes, you must have skidded off the road. You ran into a tree."

"Coll?"

"Oh yes, I called the operator to let her know to call the doctor. But I don't know if she heard me before the phone went dead."

"No, I mean Coll. Is she all right?"

She was beginning to wonder if he was a little delirious.

His dog crawled up to his face and nosed his cheek. "No, Coll, no." He lifted his hand and snapped his fingers. Instantly the dog calmed down and sat obediently.

"My name is Margie. I live here. Your dog came to tell me you were hurt."

He smiled. "Good call, Coll."

Margie cocked her head. "Call?"

"For collie. Not very inventive, am I?"

Margie chuckled. "No, I suppose not."

"I'm Johnny Turner."

"It's nice to meet you, Mr. Turner. You certainly put a scare into Coll and me."

"My head hurts a bit but I think I'm okay. I walked to your door?"

"No, you were unconscious."

"But how on earth did you get me from the car into the house?"

"With lots of angelic help, I am sure. Coll pulled you on a sled and I pushed and steered and tried to keep you from rolling off."

"Well then, I guess Coll isn't hurt. That must have been quite an endeavor! You saved my life." He stopped abruptly as if speechless.

"Well, I can't say it was my normal sort of project." She smiled but his face was so serious she stopped.

"I am deeply indebted to you, Miss Margie."

With the slightest of a nod, embarrassed, Margie stood up.

"You need some food. Do you think you can sit up? If you can, perhaps we can get you next to the fire on the couch. It is too drafty on this floor. But I was unable to move you anywhere else."

He nodded and rose slowly at her direction. She helped pull him to his feet.

As they walked slowly into the living room, he surveyed the place. "This is quite a house you have."

"It's my uncle's house. I'm just staying here temporarily."

Johnny stopped to look out the window. "Looks like we're in for a big one. I would have been frozen had it not been for you. I suppose my car is buried by now."

"I'm afraid it's been nonstop."

"Where is everyone?"

"Um...well, they've gone on holiday. It's Thanksgiving, you know."

"Ah, yes it is. But you stayed behind?"

Margie sighed. Oh, well what's the use. "They left without me. I am generally not included in their plans. I am...in their way I suppose."

"Oh, I'm sorry. But no—I am not! What if you had gone? I'd still be out there buried in the snow," he said staring out the window. He weakened a little and she reached for a table to steady them both.

"Can you hold on to this table while I move the couch closer to the fire and turn it so you can see the snow?"

"You are so thoughtful, Miss Margie. Does that stand for Margaret?"

"No, Marguerite. It was the name of a favorite friend of my mother's."

"Marguerite—a beautiful name," Johnny said as if it were a melody.

Pushing the couch proved to be a chore but she carefully tried to make it look easy. He seemed concerned at her doing it without help.

She settled him in and brought one of the blankets to warm him.

"I'll go make you something to eat."

"I wish you wouldn't make such a fuss over me. I'm sure I'll be fine shortly."

"Nonsense, I'm elated to see you doing well and it is pleasant to have the company."

"Come on, Coll." Coll followed her and Margie rewarded the patient dog with some ham scraps as she fixed soup and ham sandwiches.

She made her patient a tray and encouraged him to eat and he did, heartily.

"This is delicious."

"There's plenty, so eat all you like. I'm used to making it for the family—one of the few things they appreciate me for. I call it missionary soup but I don't tell them that or they might decide they don't like it after all."

She sat in the chair next to the couch with her own soup.

"Are your parents missionaries, then?"

"No, my parents are in heaven. But my brother Jeff is a missionary in the Philippines."

"How wonderful. How long has he been there?"

"A year and seven months." She looked longingly out the window.

His countenance matched her sorrow. "You count the time."

"Yes, he and his wife, Adele, are all I have left."

They sat by the fire and shared bits and pieces of their lives until Margie stood. "Say, let's have something special. How about some spiced cider?" And she went cheerfully to the kitchen.

The smell of cinnamon and cloves wafted into the room as she carried in cups of steaming cider.

"Ah, I think I am to have a holiday after all, thanks to you, Miss Margie."

"Please, call me Margie."

"If you will call me Johnny." His smile was genuine, his words kind.

"All right, Johnny. Won't you be spending Thanksgiving with your family?"

"I have no family. The fever." His head lowered.

Was he lonely as well this holiday? "I am so sorry.

Holidays are difficult with our loved ones gone."

The phone rang sending Margie running, but it stopped before she got there. She came back disappointed.

"I didn't make it. The storm I guess. It doesn't look like we'll have a doctor anytime soon."

"I don't think I will need a doctor with your great nursing care."

"I'm just happy you're alive."

"Well, here we are, Margie, two lone souls together. At least we don't have to spend the holiday alone."

She smiled, nodding in agreement.

"My mother would have called us Pouty Pattys today."

Margie laughed. "Yes, so we should stop pouting and be thankful."

Johnny nodded. "I agree."

Margie got up and stood by the window. The wind was blowing the snow every which way.

"I can't think what I'm going to make us for Thanksgiving dinner tomorrow."

The phone rang again, and she hurried to answer it.

"Yes, yes, Uncle Thornton. The house is fine, but—. Yes, yes, I'll make sure. The snow is heavy and there's been an acci—." She was going to tell him about Johnny, but he hung up. She tried to ring the operator, but she couldn't call out.

Margie came back into the living room. "It was my uncle wanting to know if the house was all right and giving me directions."

"He only asked about the house?"

"I am nothing but an interloper to them and they treat me like one of the servants. I will be glad to be on my own. I finished school and had nowhere else to go. But I will leave as soon as I can find a position."

"Really? What kind of skills do you have?"

"I have been well-trained as a secretary."

His eyes brightened. "I am in desperate need of a secretary. Would you consider coming to work for me?"

"That sounds wonderful. What kind of business is it?" Her gloomy mood after talking to her uncle now dispelled at the hope of a position.

"It's a shipping business. I inherited it from my uncle. He called me to come work with him but before I got there he died. I know nothing about it and all I can do is try to make a go of it. The office is a shambles, that much I know. I have a lot of work ahead of me and need someone to help put the office together. I know nothing about shipping but it's all I have. When I lost my father, I lost everything except the house. The money from the sale of the house will have to carry me until I can get the business going."

Margie was thrilled at the prospect of leaving this unloving home. "This sounds like a wonderful opportunity."

"I have no idea what kind of living arrangements there might be. I figured I would be living aboard ship if nothing else. But I can let you know when I get out there. I had only a quick look when I first picked up the papers. The coast is breathtaking though. I can tell you that."

Johnny, Margie and Coll enjoyed the rest of the peaceful day, talking about God, family, and eating a small dinner.

That night, Margie lay thinking what a wonderful turn of events had come in the guise of a lonely homecoming and a terrible accident. Johnny was lonely, too. They had both suffered terrible loss. Won't this make an interesting letter to Jeff and Adele?

Chapter 3

Margie woke to see brilliant light piercing between the curtains. Was it her own elation at not being alone today or just the snowy reflections she was seeing? She opened the curtains fully. Oh, the glory! The snow sparkled on everything from the top of the tree branches to the yard below as if it had been dusted like a sugar cookie. She pulled herself away, readied herself, and quickly prayed for the day. She picked up her Bible and went down to see her new patient and friend, who hopefully would soon be her new boss.

She popped down the stairs a bit unladylike but couldn't seem to help herself. There was hope in her heart.

Coll met her at the bottom of the stairs wagging her tail in greeting. She reached for her, gave her the attention she desired, and peeked into the parlor. Johnny wasn't on the couch, his blanket folded. Coll led her into the kitchen where she found Johnny making a fire in the stove.

"Good morning," she said.

"Yes, it is. Good morning."

"I guess you're feeling better."

He nodded and turned from the stove. His smile matched the sparkling snow, making her smile back.

"The snow was beautiful this morning, the way the sun danced upon its drifts," she said.

"It sounds like poetry putting it that way. Let's have a look." He gave her his arm and they went to the window.

They stood like children wondering at the blanket of sparkly perfection that had been spread over the earth and trees.

"He washes white as snow," Johnny said.

"He does. And I'm so glad."

"Yes, and I cannot imagine how I would have made it through these last years without the Lord. Several years ago, I made my full commitment to the Savior, no longer hanging on to my mother's apron strings so to speak," Johnny said.

"I think that happened for me when my family and friends died so quickly to the fever," Margie explained. "It pushed me closer to the Lord and away from my own ambitions."

There appeared to be true concern in his countenance as Johnny's eyes focused on her. The

20

tenderness took her breath away. It had been so long since anyone cared about her.

"It seems we have both suffered much loss," he said, then turned to look back out the window. "Do you think God brought us together on this day so we wouldn't have to be alone?"

"I suppose he did. I think we can come up with some sort of Thanksgiving meal."

A boyish grin spread across Johnny's face, making her want to laugh.

Even Coll barked in agreement.

In no time, they scavenged about the cellar, diligently trying to find the best substitute Thanksgiving they could.

"I remember seeing pumpkins in the garden. Cook must have stored them down here somewhere."

They found several things and started up the stairs. At the top of the stairs Margie heard the side door creak. She bit her bottom lip. She couldn't imagine who it could be.

She slowly pushed open the cellar door, hearing rustling boots and snow being brushed off. Margie came out into the open to see Dahlia.

"Dahlia, whatever are you doing here?"

"Miss Margie, I couldn't leave you here alone on Thanksgiving and I have no one myself so here I am, although it sure was a hard journey getting back here."

"I am so glad! I have so much to tell you," Margie said.

Just then Johnny appeared out of the cellar, with pumpkin in hand, and Coll hurried over, startling Dahlia.

"It's all right, Dahlia. It's a long story, but we have a Thanksgiving guest. Dahlia, this is Mr. Johnny Turner."

"How do you do?" Dahlia said.

"It is nice to meet you, Miss Dahlia. I am here by way of an accident and your kind friend saved my life."

Dahlia looked at Johnny, then at Margie, waiting for an explanation.

Margie led Dahlia to the fireplace to get warm. She and Johnny told the full story, while Dahlia shook her head in amazement. Then the three of them took to planning a Thanksgiving dinner.

Dahlia rubbed her hands by the fire. "Well, I can tell you there is no turkey to be found."

"We knew that much. But we'll make a delicious meal with what we have."

Just then Coll ran to the door, whining. She ran back and forth between the window and the door. Margie looked at Dahlia. She knew they were both thinking the same thing. Is it the family? Margie couldn't seem to move. Her heart sank.

Johnny looked at her with a wondering look and then turned to Coll. "What has you all stirred up, Coll?"

He went to the window but saw nothing, so he followed Coll to the front door.

Oh, don't let them in! Margie's heart cried. But of course he should and he would but she so didn't want it to happen. Their lovely holiday would be spoiled.

Johnny couldn't get the door open fast enough for Coll. She nudged past him and squeezed out to the snow-laden porch. She ran straight for a small pile at the bottom of the steps.

Margie stood petrified as Johnny reached down and picked up what appeared to be a child.

"Oh, dear." Margie raised her hand to her mouth fearing the worst.

"He hasn't been there long. Coll was just out there a little while ago," Johnny said, carrying the child in by the fire.

"I'm so tired. I couldn't find it. I don't know where it is," the boy said over and over, as Johnny carried him in by the fire.

"Margie, do you think you could find some socks like you found for me?" Johnny said.

"Yes, of course." Margie scurried up the stairs wondering where the boy had come from. Morbid thoughts ran through her head. Will he be all right? Did God send Johnny and Dahlia here so she wouldn't have to face this boy's death alone? The memories of death gripped her unmercifully. She couldn't seem to stop them.

When she came back down, Johnny was holding the boy close to him. Was he dead? She looked at Johnny's face. He was smiling. She let out the breath she had been holding.

"He's only asleep. Poor lad was exhausted and, as thin as he is, I'd say he hasn't had much to eat. Other than that, I think he will be all right." Johnny's optimism calmed Margie's fears a little. "He hasn't been out in this for too long."

Dahlia went back into the kitchen to see about getting the boy something warm to eat while Margie sat on the hearth and rested. Worry and fear were exhausting. She needed to stop letting the past push her to fear about everything. It wasn't God's way.

"The boy is going to be all right," Johnny said, a bit more convincingly, obviously seeing her distress.

"I'm trying not to fear, but I have seen so much death." She looked down ashamed of herself.

"I understand," he said gently. "I have been fighting this, too. We have to give him into God's hands."

She sniffed, "But he has such a sweet face. Must we lose everyone?"

Out of the corner of her eye Margie saw Dahlia standing near. She came and knelt next to Margie and held her hand. "From what I understand, we have all three faced this more than we should have in our lives."

"You, too, Dahlia?" Johnny asked, frowning.

"Yes, sir. I am alone. My family was small but they are all gone."

"Well, at least I have Jeff and Adele, if God sees fit to bring them back to me someday."

"I sense a bit of bitterness in those words, Margie." Johnny spoke gently, but it convicted Margie nonethelesss.

"I know. I feel angry at times," Margie said.

"I am a foolish man. I thought I was the only one in the world who had suffered and look at you two dear ladies. It is good God brought us together."

Then he asked if he might pray and they heartily agreed. *"Father in heaven, we ask you to please bring life back into this young lad. We know our loved ones are with you and we must stay the course down here. Forgive us our resentment at that. We have all felt it at times, but we have also committed all things into your hands. Our lives are not our own. We gave them to you. Help take away the fears and the pain."*

Somewhere in the middle of Johnny's prayer the boy aroused. The movement caused Margie to open her eyes. She saw the boy's eyes open and look intently into Johnny's face that was lifted upward to heaven. She smiled and waited. Johnny looked down at the end of his prayer.

"Why, hello, son, how are you feeling?" Johnny

laughed. A joyous laugh, deep and wonderful, like her poppa used to laugh.

Dahlia and Margie squeezed each other's hands in delight, waiting for the boy to talk.

"Where am I? I am dreaming. Are you my new dad?" the boy said.

"No, you are not dreaming. I am not your dad but a friend," Johnny said.

Margie stood closer. "This is my uncle's house. We found you in the snow."

"And we're so glad you're all right." Dahlia clasped her hands, smiling at the boy.

"What's your name, lad?" Johnny asked.

"Chipper, sir."

"Well, Chipper, I am glad you are here. Where do you live?" Johnny asked.

The boy hesitated. He lowered his eyes. "The Children's Home."

"What brought you all the way out here?" Margie asked.

His brows furrowed as his blue eyes seemed to trace his memory. "I was delivering something…"

"I am Johnny, this is Miss Dahlia and Miss Margie, who, by the way, is the nurse around here. You must do as she says and you'll get well. It has worked for me."

"How do you do?" Chipper said.

"We do fine now that you are awake," Dahlia said.

"And I'm heating some soup and making biscuits for you."

The boy's eyes popped. When Johnny asked him if he was hungry, he nodded, profusely.

Coll walked over to the boy. "Wow! That is a real dog."

"Yes, she is a real lifesaver. She was the one who told us you were out there in the snow," Johnny said.

"Really?"

"Yes," Margie said. "She's a treasure."

"And she and Miss Margie saved my life, for I was unconscious in the snow just like you, only in my car."

"She did? I wish I could have a dog like that."

Johnny sat Chipper on the couch as Dahlia brought a tray with soup." The biscuits are almost ready."

Chipper ate his soup and commented that Coll was a funny name for a dog. "Is that because she comes when you call?"

"No, it's because she is a collie. I just shortened the name."

Chipper looked to be about ten but he was slight and his clothes were shabby. Margie wondered at his care. "Were you going to have Thanksgiving dinner somewhere, Chipper?"

"No ma'am, I wasn't going to get Thanksgiving dinner, because I didn't finish all my errands in time."

"Oh," Margie said, saddened that they would treat

the boy so cruelly.

Johnny frowned and Margie hated to see it.

"Well, we're planning dinner and since you are stuck here with us, I suppose you'll have to join us." Margie smiled at Chipper.

"Will there be any pie?"

"Oh yes, we will have lots of pie but I am afraid we won't be having turkey."

"Turkey...turkey! Oh the turkey!" Chipper slipped from the couch and went for the door, Coll following after.

"Wait, where are you going?" Margie said, as Johnny went after him.

He stood at the door and turned to them. "I was delivering a turkey and I got lost. It must be out there in the snow."

"You stay here. Coll and I will go look for it," Johnny said, slipping on his coat and scarf and going out into the yard.

Margie wasn't comfortable with her biggest patient being out in the snow, either.

"I think I remember where I dropped it," Chipper said.

"Show me," Margie said slipping into her coat and scarf.

"It's by the front fence. I remember coming in the gate and dropping it. I was so tired walking in the snow and I got lost."

"Snow blind. You poor dear." She reached for him and gave him a quick hug. "Close the door and watch from the window. We don't want you to get cold."

She stepped into the big holes that Johnny made with his feet. But the snow was so deep, she could barely manage making her way to the fence. How did Chipper even make it to the steps? As she got closer, she called out to Johnny who was already outside the gate. He turned and saw her and came back toward her.

"What are you doing out here, Margie?"

"Chipper remembered where he dropped the turkey." She pointed. "By the gate, in the front. Please hurry. You are still a patient you know."

"We should have stopped to pray," he said, as he drew closer to her.

She nodded and he sent up a quick prayer to find it quickly. When she looked up, Johnny was looking at her intently. She could hardly speak, let alone breathe.

Then he turned toward the fence gate trying to keep his bearings, but it set her off balance. He caught her, just in time, wrapping his arms around her. But the uneven snow made them both fall. She felt his cheek as it brushed against hers. Is this what it feels like to be held by a man? It felt wonderful and so warm even in the snow. It seemed neither of them wanted to move—at least until Coll started barking.

Johnny gently helped her back up. She thanked him but then he started laughing. Why was he laughing? Margie looked around and saw Coll. She was dragging the turkey up to the front porch, and Chipper was at the window jumping up and down. Dahlia stood next to him with her mouth open. Margie and Johnny walked slowly and joyfully back to the house, her arm hooked into his. It felt so right being with him. Kindness exuded from him along with strength. Perhaps he wasn't always like this. She wondered how much of his qualities came from his loss. Suffering seems to mold God's children into his image.

Dahlia was ecstatic, clapping her hands. "Now we can have a real Thanksgiving."

"Coll, you are the greatest," Chipper said, drying the dog off.

Chapter 4

Margie sat at the servants' table, chopping celery and thinking how her whole life had changed in one day. Her heart was happy as she thought about the friends God had put together. She looked up at Johnny.

Oh Father, I long to be married to a man like Johnny someday, but now I would be happy to be his secretary. Please make a way.

The happy group sat around the table working and visiting. Johnny had split the giant Hubbard squash for Dahlia outside. It took some tough whacks with the axe but she was delighted. "I thought we were going to have to drag it to the attic and drop it out the window. I am so glad you were feeling well enough to do it."

They all laughed at the little blonde's spirited acting out of hauling the giant squash up the stairs. Margie couldn't remember the last time she laughed like this. She almost couldn't stop. Johnny's deep laugh and Chipper's giggle made her laugh all the more. She wondered how much Chipper got to laugh at the orphan's home? At his age he should be fishing and building tree houses, and being nurtured by a loving mother and father. It reminded her of how much she felt like an orphan in this house. Why did all their loved ones have to be taken when they all needed them so?

I don't always understand your ways, Father. I know you love us but I do get muddled with these kinds of questions.

They spent much of the day happily making piecrusts, carrying in wood, chopping nuts, stirring scrumptious smelling concoctions, and sharing stories of home lives long past with loved ones long gone.

They even set the table together and when they did, Johnny stopped and looked toward heaven. "What manner of God we have to bring us our missing turkey and give us all a Thanksgiving dinner that none of us would have had otherwise."

Then Dahlia's beautiful, clear voice began to sing and they all joined in except for Chipper who hummed along.

We gather together to ask the Lord's blessing;
He chastens and hastens His will to make known.
The wicked oppressing now cease from distressing.
Sing praises to His Name; He forgets not His own.

Tears seemed to glisten in Chipper's eyes.

"Are you all right, Chipper? Do you know the song?"

"Yes, Ma'am. My mother used to sing it to me. I learned it in Dutch."

"How wonderful. That's the original language, isn't it?" Margie asked.

"Yes, Ma'am."

"Please sing it for us. We'll hum along."

Chipper's neck jerked a bit as it seemed to do when he became nervous, but nevertheless he started to sing.

Wilt heden nu treden voor God den Heere,
Hem boven al loven van herten seer,
End' maken groot zijns lieven namens eere,
Die daar nu onsen vijan slaat terneer.

His voice was amazing and they all cheered, making him grin and turn red. He was such a lovable boy.

"Oh, Chipper, your mother would be so pleased," Margie said, giving Chipper a warm hug and trying desperately not to start her own flood of tears.

"That was a real blessing, lad," Johnny said. "You have a wonderful voice. My mother used to flinch a bit when I sang." His deep laugh surfaced again and kept them all from tears for the boy's loss.

Margie smiled at Johnny. His voice may be a bit off key, but she loved it just the same.

At the stove, Margie stirred and daydreamed.

Wouldn't it be wonderful to be a family? She and Johnny, Chipper, Dahlia and Coll? She swirled her thoughts into the cranberry sauce so she couldn't be caught with them in her heart. But they lingered, for when she looked up, Johnny was looking at her with those eyes—eyes that melted her right into the cranberry sauce and left her cheeks most likely matching its color.

After it was cooked, Margie grabbed Dahlia's hand. "Let's go get dressed for dinner." They giggled all the way up the stairs to the attic, neither of them having even a speck of fun in ages. Margie gave Dahlia her nicest dress and the two preened for dinner. Dahlia was perfect in Margie's light blue silk and Margie in her mauve with the cream-colored lace that lay across her shoulders and up her neck. They tidied their hair and left.

When they came downstairs, they were met with admiring stares. Even Coll sat politely with her head cocked.

"Wow! You look real pretty," Chipper said.

"Indeed," Johnny said, making Margie pinch her lips together trying not to smile. There was something about the way he looked at her.

The table was set as for royalty and with an elegant crystal bowl in the middle filled with giant maple leaves that Johnny and Chipper had retrieved from the snow, when Margie had told them earlier how she and her

34

mother used to take the most perfect red maple leaves and make a centerpiece for the Thanksgiving table. Johnny whispered to Chipper. They went out the side door and surprised her with rich red leaves.

The friends were happily chattering when Coll, who had bedded down in the corner, perked her ears and jumped up. Margie's breath caught. Not now! Her relatives couldn't possibly come home in this snow, could they?

Margie suddenly lost her appetite as Dahlia went to the door. Margie stood and braced for battle. What would she say if it was her family? How would she explain?

But there was a knock. Her family would never knock. Dahlia opened the door to a thin somewhat grey-haired man. Margie hoped it wasn't someone from the orphanage.

"Hello, sorry it took so long to get here."

Dahlia stared at the man not saying a word for a long time before finally asking him to come in.

"Well, where's the patient?"

Johnny and Margie looked at each other and Margie started to laugh. The old man looked around confused, which made Margie laugh even more.

Johnny smiled and helped the man out of his coat. "It seems, Doctor, your patients have recovered."

"Is that so? That's a relief. I've had quite a time

getting around in this snow," the doctor said.

"Oh, Doctor, I'm so sorry. I didn't mean to laugh. It's a long story, but if you join us for dinner we'll explain. Have you had dinner?" Margie said.

"As a matter of fact, I don't believe I've eaten since yesterday sometime," the doctor said, scratching his forehead.

"Oh dear. Then you must come and sit. We have prepared quite a meal today," Johnny said.

"We had no way to contact you to let you know that our patients seem to be fine now," Margie said.

The doctor washed up, and they set a place at the table for him. "I am Dr. Truen, Theodore Truen. Folks call me Doc."

"Welcome to our not-so-lonely Thanksgiving dinner, Doc," Johnny said, grinning.

"Yes sir, we are mostly all strangers," Margie explained.

"Really? How did you manage that?" Doc asked.

So they told him the amazing stories of the last two days.

Doc shook his head. "Now I know for sure the Lord has a sense of humor. And you young men, you are feeling fine?"

Chipper nodded. "I got lost and tired out in the snow. These folks have taken great care of me."

"And I feel perfectly fine, thanks to all the nursing

care I received," Johnny said smiling at Margie.

"I do believe it sounds like some Thanksgiving miracles happened here. I should've had more faith, that's what my wife used to always tell me," Doc said.

Dahlia interrupted. "The food is getting cold. Shall we say grace?" She nodded to Johnny.

"Father, what a glorious, strange set of events that has brought us all together to this table. A plan orchestrated by your hand for a group of lonely souls who needed cheering up on this Thanksgiving holiday. Thank you, Father, for all we have been given and all we have before us, knowing you have created this meeting, and you will bless it. Thank you so very much, Lord."

"That was beautiful and so true. He has done this," Margie said.

"Yes, the best Thanksgiving I've had since I was home," Chipper said.

They all agreed.

"How is it you are all alone in this huge house, my dear?" Doc asked.

"My parents died and I came here to stay with my uncle's family. They had taken their holiday elsewhere," Margie said.

"My family is gone as well," Johnny said.

"And mine, even my baby sister," Chipper said, lowering his head.

"Mine have been gone for a long time," Dahlia said.

"My wife was taken by the fever. I...I couldn't save her," Doc said, solemnly.

For a few moments, they seemed to mourn together then slowly began to pass the food around. As they did their faces brightened and they began to enjoy the meal for the blessing it was meant to be.

"The Bible says that he sets the lonely in families. Perhaps that is what he has accomplished on this snowy but sunny Thanksgiving Day," Johnny said.

"It does? It says that?" Chipper asked, eyes full of wonder.

Margie nodded. "Yes, Chipper. That is in Psalms isn't it, Johnny?"

"Yes, it is. I'm not sure which psalm, but I will look it up later," Johnny said.

The meal proved to be perfect and even if it hadn't been, it was perfect to them because it was something they had not enjoyed in a long time. The golden roasted turkey, the creamy mashed potatoes, the buttery dark squash and all the rest filled them up, barely making room for the beautiful pies Dahlia and Margie created with help from Johnny and Chipper.

As the pies were served, Doc lifted his glass of water and stood. "To this lovely Thanksgiving family that the Lord brought together today, may we all consider each other in the years to come and remember God's miracles."

As they enjoyed their desserts, the story of Coll finding the turkey brought new laughter to the table. The camaraderie was strong, the laughter heartening— until Coll started to bark at the door.

Chapter 5

The door flew open and Margie's uncle and aunt with eyes wide and mouths open, stepped into the house.

A loud screech came from her aunt. "A dog!"

"What is the meaning of this?" Margie's uncle stormed to the edge of the table, his eyes blazing.

Margie stood up instantly as did all of her guests.

"Uncle Thornton, please, these are my friends. I... I wasn't expecting you back so soon."

"Friends? Friends, you have no friends," her uncle said disdainfully, boring holes into the faces of each of them, his large jowls flopping at he spoke.

Johnny and Doc quickly jumped to her defense.

Doc spoke first. "Sir, we are sorry to impose. We had quite an ordeal here you see."

Her uncle started to listen, then turned to the dog. "Why is there a dog in my house?" he said with gritted teeth.

"Please sir, we've had an accident here in the storm and we were just trying to have a meal together," Doc said.

"Yes, sir. I'm afraid I became unconscious when I slid off the road and hit a tree —" Johnny started.

"Unconscious? Were you drunk?" Uncle Thorton's voice boomed over every explanation. It was clear he was not going to listen.

"Oh, no. I don't drink, sir, I —" Johnny said, with his hand on Coll.

Margie's eyes pooled with tears. She couldn't stand for her friends to be treated so. "Uncle Thornton, these people were stuck in the snow and two of them could have died."

"Hmph. I suppose you wanted to pay us back for leaving you, so you picked this group up on your own."

As Dahlia came forward, he scowled at her. "What are you doing here?"

"I didn't want to leave Miss Margie alone, sir."

"I suppose some of these people are your ragamuffin friends." Turning to Chipper, he continued his rant. "Where are you from, boy?"

"The Children's Home," Chipper mumbled.

"See! I knew it, they have probably stolen us blind," Margie's aunt said, coming from behind.

Doc's brow furrowed, his face reddening by the second. Margie started over to protect Chipper, but the boy ran out the door. Johnny took Coll out and Doc retrieved his medical case.

"I have never been accused of such evil things," Doc mumbled as he started to leave. He turned to her uncle. "Sir, your injustice and bad behavior will not go unnoticed by the Almighty. I hope you haven't sent that poor lad off to his doom after being just rescued from the cold."

Margie looked at Dahlia and they were both in tears. Dahlia stayed to clear the table and Margie ran outside after her friends.

"I...I..." Margie tried to talk but the words wouldn't come.

"It's all right, child. I am sure your uncle will calm soon and best if we leave so he can," Doc said.

A honking car slipped and slid up the driveway and the cousins piled out. Margie cowered.

"Say, what's this all about, cuz? Partying while the cat's away? I bet Father is in a stew. He was already boiling mad when we missed the last train," Lala said.

"Gee, Margie, as if being stuck in the attic and doing servant's chores wasn't bad enough. You might get tossed out in the barn now," Geri said, making Lala laugh.

Margie tried to ignore her rude cousins and followed her friends out the gate, wishing desperately she was going with them. At least she had Dahlia, who was most likely being reprimanded right now.

"Doc, I don't think there is anything I can do about my car right now. Do you think I could get a lift into town?" Johnny asked.

"I think we can manage in the sleigh," Doc said.

"I am so sorry, so very sorry." Margie had done it now. Speaking had made fountains pour down her cheeks.

"Oh, no," Johnny said, reaching for her hand. "We are sorry for all of this. But it doesn't appear we could have done anything to appease them."

"No, there is no pleasing them. They resent me and I can do nothing about it but I have no recourse."

Johnny squeezed her hand and she wanted him to never let go. "I wish I could bring you right now but I have no place for you to live. It is rather a rural spot on the edge of the sea. But I will come for you as soon as I am able."

After exchanging addresses with Doc and Johnny, Margie looked down the road after Chipper. "I hope you find him."

"Coll will sniff him out," Johnny said, his eyes filled with compassion. Coll nuzzled her and it reminded her of Pepper.

"Tell Chipper goodbye and I am sorry, please."

Johnny nodded. They said their goodbyes and blessed her over and over for her generosity and asked her to thank Dahlia for them.

Margie watched them go, waving and wishing so badly she could leave with them. She turned to go back to the house and face her persecutors. Looking up, she saw Dahlia on the second floor wiping at her eyes. Margie's own tears started dripping again and she realized she still had Johnny's handkerchief. She held it close to her heart like a treasure.

"There he is!" Johnny jumped off as soon as Doc slowed the sleigh. Coll had already bailed out, running for the boy.

"Chipper, Chipper, over here!"

The boy saw Johnny and started toward him, Coll now at his side. Johnny ran and scooped him up. He was like ice. He sat the shivering boy into the sleigh and wrapped him in a blanket Doc had waiting. They squeezed him in-between them for more warmth. Coll curled in the floorboard of the sleigh and they were off.

"You all right, son?" Doc asked.

"Yessir. I am now," Chipper chattered.

They set off speedily through the snow-packed landscape toward town. The last sun rays were starting to peek through the trees, sending messages to hurry because darkness was lurking, waiting for its turn.

"Why did you run off?" Johnny asked.

"I guess I was scared he'd come and tell the headmaster, and I would be without food for days."

Johnny looked at Doc, horrified. "They don't feed you if you are in trouble?"

"No food. Usually the other kids will give me a little something but they could end up in the same stew if they got caught. I try hard to keep my nose clean. You know what I mean, right?"

"Yes, I understand." Johnny felt beyond helpless today. Leaving poor Margie and Dahlia to fend with the ogre uncle and now poor Chipper. His heart broke for the boy. He must make this shipping business good so he could give Margie a job and find a way to help Chipper.

"Do you have friends at the home, lad?" Johnny asked.

"A few, but some went into the factories once they were eleven. My only true friend was little Doug. He is small so I try to protect him from the bullies. But he is being adopted."

"Well, that is happy for Doug, isn't it? Perhaps we should pray for you to be adopted," Johnny said.

"Likely won't do much good. I am too old and scrawny. They usually want a boy to work for them, not to be their kid."

Chipper's predicament was wearing hard on Johnny. He wished he could just take the boy home and be done with it, but there were laws against such things.

Eventually, Chipper fell asleep and they made their way to Doc's house just as the last rays of the sunset dimmed.

"Oh good, my housekeeper, Lottie, has a fire going. The house will be nice and warm." Doc looked up at the smoke coming from the chimney. "She usually cooks me out of the house with the heat, but tonight I am glad."

"I'll see to the horse, Doc, as soon as I get Chipper in," Johnny said carrying the sleeping boy inside.

"Thank you, son."

"Oh, Doc, I was so worried about you," A fairly plump woman greeted them. "Oh dear, is the boy ill?"

Chipper woke and stood up, a little groggy.

"No, he is fine. Just got lost...and found." Doc winked at Chipper.

"Well, that is good news. All the Shumate family is sick and the Mosiers are beside themselves with Grandpa Mosier having a seizure. I took some food to the Thompsons, but they weren't very receptive and I don't know why since I had given them a jar of my prize jam last time. Oh, and little Mara Wheatley is having some strong colic and ..."

Johnny saw to the horse and when he came back, a hot meal awaited him. He wasn't sure how Lottie managed it since she seemed to have not stopped talking since their arrival. Poor Doc. That could get old.

"Thank you, Lottie. I am sure Doc Anderson took care of it all. These are my friends, Johnny and Chipper."

"Oh, nice to meet ya. Is he your boy? Looks like he needs some food to fatten him up. Here Chip, have some bread."

"Lottie, we need to discuss a few things, if you don't mind," Doc said gently, but with an authority she seemed to be used to.

"Yes, Doc."

The talkative woman shut up and went back into the kitchen. Doc didn't say word. He just looked up and winked at Johnny and Chipper. Doc seemed to know how to handle her. It appeared they all had their burdens. He only wished he knew how to lighten them.

Finally after finishing his stew, Doc looked up. "Gentleman, there is no use going out at this late hour. If you don't mind bedding down here and there, we can accommodate you."

"Thank you, Doc. We are grateful," Johnny answered.

Chipper nodded. Johnny was sure the boy was glad for one more day away from the orphan's home.

He started to think about Margie and Dahlia and what kind of an evening they were having. Would Margie have to put up with more from her angry family?

Yes, he thought so. He frowned at such a thought. What a lovely time they spoiled for the happy group of Thanksgiving visitors.

Johnny cut himself out of his daydream, realizing Doc was talking to him. "Oh I'm sorry. What were you saying?"

"Only that you seemed somewhere else for a moment," Doc said.

"Yes I suppose I was. I'm afraid I was thinking of our poor lovely hostesses. Somehow I feel they'd be happier to be here with us having stew instead of being in a stew with that family."

"They're a sour bunch. But Miss Margie is not like them. She's a peach," Chipper said.

The older man laughed. "Yes and Miss Dahlia, too. Such lovely young ladies and so kind."

"Say, Mr. Johnny, I saw you looking at Miss Margie. You ought to marry her."

Doc winked at Chipper.

A little embarrassed, Johnny ate his stew. He hadn't let marriage cross his thoughts at all until he met Margie. What was it about her? Dahlia was also beautiful but Margie seemed more suited for him. She was the kind of girl he wanted to marry one day. But first he had to get his business up and running. He needed a focused mind to do it.

"Well, right now, Chipper, I think I had better

48

provide the girl a position so she can get out of that sour bunch's house as you called them."

"That is a great idea, son. What kind of position can you afford her?" Doc asked.

"I need a secretary and quickly but I have nowhere to house her. I inherited my uncle's shipping business and it is in ruins. I went there once and it will take every ounce of my energy and brains to get it running. People there on the coast counting on me to hire them as well. But," he added, "first I need to retrieve my car."

"Tomorrow I will take you by Mack's place. He owes me a lot, so he will get your car running for you," Doc said.

"Snow's supposed to melt tomorrow," Lottie said, coming in with apple cobbler.

"That's good to know," Johnny said.

"Thank you, Lottie. This cobbler looks delicious," Doc said.

Johnny felt Doc must be rather gracious for the cobbler looked rather burnt and tasted pretty awful. But Chipper didn't seem to mind at all.

"Chipper, do you have a resident doctor at the Children's Home?" Doc asked.

"Yessir, and he is cranky. He doesn't like kids, even the girls."

Johnny was saddened by the way the orphanage was run. He wondered if someday there could be something he could do for all these children. Perhaps, when they took Chipper home Johnny would be able to see the state of the orphanage for himself.

The three retired and Johnny could hear distant snores from Doc and light ones from Chipper in the room. But sleep escaped him because every time he closed his eyes he saw the beautiful surprised eyes that met him when he came to himself after the accident. How daring Margie was, taking it upon herself to drag him into the house. He didn't know how she managed it. But he was alive because of her and he would do everything in his power to help her. One thing he didn't understand was this desire that made him long to see her again— and soon.

He also thought about what Chipper said—Margie being a peach and all and how Johnny should marry her. Then it dawned on him, Chipper must have seen the way he looked at her. Was he that obvious? But he wasn't sure he wanted to love anyone again only to lose them and have their memories piercing his heart. It was too hard. No, he couldn't. Not yet, anyway. But if he ever did...

Chapter 6

How one could be so extremely lonely in the middle of a big family escaped Margie, but she was. She sat in her small attic room and daydreamed about the taste of a warm Thanksgiving dinner with Johnny, Dahlia, Doc, Chipper, and Coll in the corner waiting patiently for scraps. Poor Chipper, scared off by her insensitive uncle.

Father, I pray that they found little Chipper and he is safe. Please send someone to love him and adopt him. I pray for Johnny's business that all would go well and quickly. I also pray that there would be a place for me to go and be a part of it. But even if not, please still bless him for he is a good and kind man and he loves you. Take care of Doc and his loneliness. Help him not to miss his wife so much, Father, and keep Dahlia and me as we live in this house with people who do not care for us nor for you.

Chipper was such a good-natured boy but so thin and working so hard. It made her heart sad. And there

51

was Doc, missing his wife and working too much at his age. Then her mind came to Johnny. Dear gentle, deep-voiced, handsome Johnny. She sighed. Just thinking about him made her feel hopeful. There was nothing she did that didn't take her back to that precious Thanksgiving with him. When he caught her and they fell in the snow, his arms were so comforting. But he was so charming, kind, godly and—too perfect for the likes of her. Besides there was Amy, whose touching valentine card was in his pocket. Why didn't he mention her? Best to keep praying and not be overly hopeful, but if there weren't any hope, how would she manage?

She missed her real family and she missed her makeshift family. She missed Pepper and she missed Coll. Now she had lost twice. No! I won't believe that lie. I believe we will all be together again.

Please help my unbelief.

Margie had just removed her shoes when the familiar sound of clomping heels accosted her peace. Then she heard the whining sound of Nettie's voice.

"Margie, come down and help me. I spilled all my beads and they're all over the floor."

Margie rolled her eyes. Spoiled cousins. Were they all so helpless? They didn't even want to bend over to pick up their own messes. She reached for her shoes, but Nettie grabbed her arm, pulling her off the bed, the momentum carrying them both down the attic stairs.

Margie closed her eyes when she saw the beads strewn all over the floor. It didn't make the irritating scene go away. How had Nettie managed this? Picking up the beads was going to take some time and she was so weary. She scanned the colors. They were mostly red.

"You pick up the red ones, Nettie, and I'll do the yellow." Nettie wasn't particularly clever. Perhaps Margie could get away with it.

Nettie blinked at her and the spoiled girl's jaw dropped. "Me? Why should I pick them up?"

"Perhaps because you were the one who spilled them?" Margie did not want to be bullied into the job.

"But, but —"

Margie tried to take control. "Now grab the empty vase on your dresser and let's get this done."

"But —" The spoiled child was not used to being told what to do, but Margie coaxed her to help.

However, Margie ended up collecting three times the beads of her lazy cousin and groveled under the bed to get many of them.

"This is so annoying," Nettie complained. "Perhaps I should have called Dahlia to help me."

Oh, no. Not wanting poor Dahlia to do this work, Margie started doing some of the red ones, too. Then she stood up with hands on her hips and dared the girl to do anything but finish her own red beads. It was too late to bother Dahlia.

"Good night, Nettie." Margie turned to go up the stairs knowing she would probably pay for this the next day with reprimands from her aunt, but she was too tired to care. All she wanted to do was just lie on her bed and reminisce about the wonderful time she had spent with her Thanksgiving friends—and to dream about working for Johnny.

After getting ready for bed, she climbed into the cold sheets, but happily shivered as she could now rest and think about happier times. She recalled the last two days as if they were a lifetime of happiness. She must write Jeff and tell him, and she must write her apologies to her friends. Oh, but Johnny had no address right now. Well, he would write, and soon. She was sure of it.

At breakfast, the fiasco began.

"And she didn't even help me with the beads! She knew I could slip and fall but she was too tired." Nettie's whine began.

Margie's aunt drew a breath. "That certainly was rude, Marguerite, not helping your poor cousin."

"I did —"

"No, she didn't. She only picked up the yellow ones and there weren't as many of them."

Margie knew it was hopeless defending herself to them.

"I would think you would have more concern

regarding your behavior young lady after all the shenanigans you pulled this week."

Margie watched as the rest joined the bandwagon until she couldn't eat one more bite.

Ralston was the only silent juror. He was usually too hungover to say much at breakfast. She only gave a fleeting look to Nettie, who looked away and guiltily turned red.

As a sheep to the slaughter... Well, not quite that bad, Lord, but I certainly feel beaten down.

Then she proceeded to clear the table. Why they hadn't banned her to the servants' table in the kitchen, she had no idea. It was one thing she really wished they would do. At least she could eat in peace and be treated kindly.

After cleaning the table and helping Dahlia with the dishes, Margie grabbed her coat and hat and went outside into the cold. The memory that warmed her lured her out the little gate to see Johnny's car. Would she see him when he came for it?

Her heart rejoiced at the memory of being able to save his life, along with the help of sweet Coll. The memory of poor Chipper running out because of her uncle's tirade brought tears to her eyes. What was his little world like at the orphanage? She couldn't imagine.

She tried to forgive her harsh, ungrateful family that lived an absurd existence in that house. She stood looking back at the house. Except for Dahlia, there was no one, and they kept her so busy Margie hardly saw her.

Lord, I wish I never had to walk through that door again. They're horrid—the whole bunch of them. But I know I must forgive them, but I always forgive them and they never change. Ever.

Margie continued to pray until she worked through forgiveness yet again. Then she went back toward the house.

"Well, that's idiotic—going out into the cold," Geri said, as she lounged across the sofa with a magazine.

Margie ignored her and hung up her coat.

"I should think you'd be up making the beds, Margar-eete."

Oh, Lord, I just forgave them and now this. I need your help to do this. Please deliver me from this house of mockers!
AND THEY SHALL MOCK HIM, AND SHALL SCOURGE HIM, AND SHALL SPIT UPON HIM, AND SHALL KILL HIM: AND THE THIRD DAY HE SHALL RISE AGAIN.

Oh! You faced them, too, of course. Forgive me, Lord. You forgave them, I can forgive this family.

Chapter 7

This is deplorable! How could any child live in such a place? Keeping his thoughts and emotions to himself, Johnny sat staring at a ramshackle building with children being lined up to work. Some were being carted away to who knows where.

Chipper waved at a friend who sat in the back of a wagon. "That's Kip. He's a good fellow. He works all day long at the wood mill for nothing. All his money goes to Mr. Bickers. Everyone's does."

"What do you do, Chipper?" Doc asked.

"I am an errand boy until I get to be eleven or so, then I'll go to the wood mill most likely. Maybe sooner." Chipper hung his head.

"Which man is Mr. Bickers?" Johnny said.

"There—in the grey coat. The pudgy one with the dark black mustache."

"Well, we'll go with you and make sure all is well for you," Doc said.

"Yes, he must have been worried about you," Johnny added.

Chipper snorted. "Naw, he'd be glad. One less mouth to feed. And he calls me scrawny."

Johnny couldn't argue with the fact that the boy was slight. Nonetheless he and Doc escorted the young boy to his master and tried to explain what happened.

"So did you deliver the turkey?" the headmaster asked.

"Uh, no sir, I couldn't because of the storm," Chipper said.

The man stood stone cold, his squinty blue eyes glaring at the boy. "Likely story. You'll be working double time for that."

"Sir, the boy has been under duress. He was found delirious and freezing in the snow. He would've been dead, if this man's dog had not found him." Doc was getting angrier by the moment, and so was Johnny.

"Sir, what was the amount Chipper was to receive for the turkey?" Johnny asked.

"He was supposed to bring back $4.75."

Chipper's head popped up slightly and his head began to jerk as it did whenever he was nervous.

"Chipper, was that the price?" Johnny whispered.

Chipper hedged a little but spoke back in a whisper. "Naw, it was $4.45."

But Chipper was too loud. The man heard him.

"You calling me a liar, boy?"

Johnny was sorry he asked Chipper and he quickly cut the amount that the man first spoke, knowing full well he was a cheat and yes, a liar, but was hoping to save the boy's back. The churl took it and gripped it in his fist. Johnny had an uneasy feeling the man would punish Chipper anyway.

Chipper had walked back over to Coll where some other orphans had gathered and he scratched the dog's head. Coll nuzzled himself into the boy's chest. "Bye Coll, I'm going to miss you."

Johnny followed the boy and stood watching, his heart wrenching. He wished he could load the boy into the sleigh and leave. Of course he couldn't but he made up his mind to do something for the lad.

Johnny put one hand on the boys shoulder. "You'll see us again, Chipper, and I will be praying for you and the other children."

"Thank you, sir. We sure need it." Then a little boy came up to Chipper and hugged him.

"Is this little Doug?" Johnny asked.

Chipper nodded.

"We thought you were dead, Chipper," Doug said.

"Thanks to these folks, I'm not," Chipper said.

"I'll be going to my new home. I just couldn't go without knowing you were okay." Little Doug clung to Chipper's arm.

"When are you leaving?"

The little boy put his head down. "Tomorrow."

Chipper's little mouth began to quiver and he pretended to have some dirt in his eye.

Johnny's heart broke. The poor lad's only true friend would be gone and his life would be lonelier than ever. He knew what that was like—loneliness. A deep pit where no one even tries to reach you because they have their own lives and families.

Johnny looked down. Chipper's young hand was extended toward him. He grasped it in both of his and drew the boy toward him squeezing his bony shoulders. He pushed a bill into his hand.

Chipper hesitated. Johnny put a finger to his mouth and Chipper nodded. He hoped the boy would be able to use the hidden funds for food, perhaps on his errands.

"I will write you. Will you write back?"

"Yessir, and will you tell me about your business and the sea and what Coll is doing?"

"Gladly, young friend, gladly."

The boy's eyes lit up with hope and just in time because Chipper was being aggressively summoned.

"I'll write soon." Johnny waved as Chipper took off. Perhaps the boy would be able to bear the harsh taskmaster more easily with hope in his heart.

Doc was coming toward them and bent over to tell the boy some things Johnny could not hear. Then the two men took off, too sad to speak. Even Coll laid her head on Johnny's knee.

Soon they were at Mack's garage and making arrangements to get Johnny's car. Doc said goodbye and promised to write. He said he had told Chipper he would come to see him now and again.

When Johnny and the mechanic reached the broken-down car, Johnny strained to see Margie. He searched the windows and yard. Then he saw her, hanging clothes in the side yard. He hollered her name and waved. When she saw him, she started to come but a car drove into the driveway. He clasped his folded hands together to let her know he would be praying. She nodded and did the same. What a lovely smile she had. He would carry it with him all the way to the sea.

Father, I pray you will keep these dear people—Margie, Chipper, Dahlia, and Doc. They all face hard things as they go on with their lives. I can hardly bear it. If only I could help them all somehow, someway. Will you show me?

Chapter 8

"I should think someone without home or family would be grateful for what you have been afforded here young lady!" The memory of her uncle's voice boomed in Margie's ears as loudly as when he said it weeks ago. She tried to tell him she was thankful but he wouldn't listen. Maybe she wasn't. Maybe she should be. She did have food and a place to sleep.

The guilt that her relatives poured out on her about Thanksgiving Day was beginning to torment her, but was she really guilty? Was it an evil thing she did to help save lives? She sighed. Of course not. It reminded her of the way the Pharisees harassed the Lord for healing people on the Sabbath day. It was absurd then and it is absurd now.

Would life always be this way? The thought smothered her. She must not let go of hope.

The familiar soft steps of Dahlia took her mind away from her thoughts. She popped up from her stool and greeted her.

"It's a letter for you, Miss Margie."

"Oh, thank you, Dahlia."

"And the missus said you should come down early to approve the table as there will be guests for dinner."

"What? Since when did she ask for my approval? How odd."

"I thought so, too. I wish I could stay and talk but she's keeping me very busy today."

Margie nodded and Dahlia turned to go down the steps.

Margie looked at the envelope. It wasn't from Jeff. She didn't recognize the writing. When she opened it , something dropped to the floor. It was a tiny leaf which looked dry but still vibrant in fall color. She sat it on the bed next to her and opened the letter.

Oh! It's from Johnny. She couldn't decide whether to save it for later or read it right now but she didn't think she could wait.

My Dear Friend and Lifesaver, Margie,

I hope this letter, which took far too long in coming to you, finds you well and in good health. I have so much I would like to share with you...

Margie read on through the story of finding Chipper and their staying at Doc's house. He went on to tell about the experience at the orphanage. Poor little Chipper. She laid the letter on her lap.

Oh, Father, why have I complained? Do forgive me. Dear Chipper is at the mercy of such a hard man. I am ashamed. I have so much to be thankful for.

She dabbed at her eyes so she could read the rest of the letter, wondering about Johnny and his new life and business. Would he be reunited with his Amy, the girl who sent the card in his pocket? She hoped he would be happy no matter what. Perhaps she and Amy would be great friends.

She went back to the letter…

I hesitate to tell you this but my uncle's business is a disaster. I do not know how I can restore it but I suppose I have no choice. Even if it was doing well, I couldn't send for you because I have nowhere for you to board as this is an extremely rural area of the coast.

Be assured that as soon as I am able I will send for you as I do need a secretary desperately. The files and papers are in terrible disarray. I am thinking someone may have even sabotaged it once he took ill.

I hope this doesn't bring too much disappointment to you. But please, dear friend, know assuredly that I have not for a moment forgotten you and your blessed care for me.

I pray for you daily, along with Chipper, Dahlia,

and Doc. I do believe Coll misses you too. She seems to mope around more since leaving our Thanksgiving family.

I hope you are doing well and your family has forgotten our intrusion.

Your indebted friend,
Johnny Turner

Margie didn't know whether to cry or be encouraged. His words were so kind. But sadly, it looked as if it would take forever for him to rescue her with the new job.

She walked over to the attic window, clutching his letter to her heart. Looking out, she remembered them sitting by the fireplace looking out at the snow together. What a precious time of friendship they shared. How had one short time become more to her than many other memories? Was it Johnny? No, not just Johnny and yet it was. She was mistreated but not crammed into a bed amongst lonely little souls as dear little Chipper. She hadn't lost her beloved spouse like Doc, and she wasn't faced with the formidable task of a business left in ruins. How she wished she could help but it didn't appear she would be leaving anytime soon.

She finally rested on the bed and fell asleep. When she woke, she faced the news all over again and even though sad and discouraged she made up her mind to write back promptly.

The tapping of feet on the stairs set Margie on edge. It sounded like her aunt and she scrambled to hide her precious letter.

"Marguerite, I brought this gown for you to wear for tonight's dinner. I want you to be well-dressed. What you have is far outdated and your uncle insists you make a pleasant impression. Your uncle's colleagues and their sons will be coming. You won't be cleaning tables tonight."

"All right, Aunt Millicent." She offered her aunt a chair as the woman was trying to catch her breath after climbing the stairs, her chest rising up and down. But she ignored Margie.

"And we're moving you to the far guest room of the children's wing, so pack up your things."

"Today?"

"No, tomorrow. The maid is preparing the room. And when you come down for tea, you can see to the table decorations."

Margie stood for a long time at the top of the stairwell, looking down. What was this about? A change of clothing, no cleaning tables, and her aunt had never climbed the stairs to the attic. Something was up.

She turned to the gown strewn across the bed. It was lovely. She quickly tried it on. It fit nicely, although a bit wide in the waist, but she could fix it. Turning to the cracked mirror, her eyes grew startled at her image. She turned to the left, then right, feeling like a giddy schoolgirl.

The whole scenario was odd but she shrugged her shoulders and pinned the dress.

When she went down to tea, she stopped on the second floor for a peek at her new room. Then she heard her name. Ralston's door was ajar again and she heard him talking.

"Well, I think Father wants to marry her off. Why? I have no idea."

"But why put her down here with us?" Geri said. Her prickly voice made Margie shrink back.

"Don't know. I guess so she doesn't tell any of the suitors she lives in the attic? Absurd idea anyway, putting her in the attic. Was she supposed to be treated like a mouse?"

"Well, we didn't want her down her with us," Geri said, with a huff.

As the voices came closer Margie went on down the hallway hoping to find her new room. Then it dawned on her. Suitors? What suitors?

She came to the last room and peered inside. She had never seen this room. It was lovely. She tiptoed in quietly. The large poster bed looked sumptuous. The bedposts were beautifully hand-carved and shined to perfection. An alluring invitation to rest. The sunlight came filtering through the lace curtains, making intricate designs on the wooden floor.

Dahlia scurried in behind her. "It's about time they started treating you like the princess you are, Miss Margie," she whispered as if the walls could hear.

"Oh, Dahlia, you are so sweet but we both know I am not a princess."

"You deserve the best."

"But so do you. Do you think we will be able to see each other more now?"

"Yes, because your aunt has appointed me as your personal maid."

"What? Me?" Margie laughed at the preposterous idea.

"Now, don't complain. We'll have more time together."

"I won't. That's wonderful."

"Your room will be ready soon. Oh, it's teatime."

"I suppose I do need a personal maid. I had better go."

As Margie walked back down the hallway, she forgot all about her cousins' remarks. She had a lovely room and time with her friend. Things seemed to be changing for the better.

Chapter 9

It was not at all what she was used to wearing. Margie felt awkward and yet she looked stunning. She wondered what Johnny would think.

Dahlia stood behind her with her hands on her cheeks. "Ah, you look lovely, Miss Margie."

"I'm not accustomed to wearing gowns like this."

"Yes, but it suits you."

The colors of the gown were beautiful, especially the rich, shiny green that brought out the flecks of green in her hazel eyes.

"Now sit here and let me help you with your hair before Geri calls me."

Margie sat down and between the two of them, they arranged her hair perfectly in a fashionable style.

"This suits you too," Dahlia said.

Suits. Oh no! Suitors. Margie turned around abruptly. "Dahlia, oh my, I just remembered what I heard Ralston and Geri talking about. I forgot all about it. I was so excited about my room and the two of us having more time together."

"What did they say?" Dahlia asked.

"Something about my uncle arranging for suitors for me."

Dahlia sat down on the bed, crushed. "So this is what this is all about. I should have known. I thought they had a change of heart. Silly me."

"Dahlia, can my uncle rightfully marry me off?"

"I don't know. Aren't you of age?"

"Yes I am. But I have nowhere to go and they obviously do not want me here."

Dahlia sighed, her eyes roaming to gather her thoughts.

"Dahl-i-a!" Geri's screeching cry came just as Dahlia had jumped up to see the rumbling noise from outside the window.

As Dahlia started for the door to answer Geri's cry, she grabbed Margie's hand and squeezed it. "It will be all right, I'm sure."

Margie stood at the window. I must hurry, I don't want to make an entrance. She would rather eat her dinner in the servants' quarters but that would not be the case tonight. She hurried down the stairs wishing she were going to greet Johnny and not unknown suitors.

"Marguerite!" her aunt called. "Come and sit by Geri." Geri was dressed up and did not look at all like she normally did. Her gown was very modern and not to Margie's liking. It was much too revealing.

She watched as the company filtered through the doorway chattering and into the room. The room where she and Johnny watched as fall and winter met. What a blessed time that was.

Some of Geri's friends came in and congregated by her, looking at Margie as if she were contemptuous. They whispered about her and laughed. She turned to look out the window, her only place of solace.

"Marguerite, stop looking out the window," her aunt said through gritted teeth.

Margie straightened and waited to be introduced to the company of four young men and two young women. Ralston came down the stairs. He already had a nip so he was overly friendly which was not his way unless he had indulged.

Margie sat observing, wishing she might fly to a room and hide like a little bird going back to its nest when the big birds showed up.

Uncle Thornton led two of the men over to Margie. He grinned like a Cheshire cat, something she'd never seen him do before. Why did she feel she was for sale by the highest bidder?

"Gentlemen, meet my lovely niece, Marguerite," her uncle said.

Both men descended upon her with smiles that made her shrink back against the couch. Geri let out a huge unladylike laugh that stopped both men and her uncle from their intense focus on her. She leaned over to Margie and whispered. "They won't bite."

Uncle Thornton gave a snort at his bitingly sarcastic daughter and walked back to the other guests.

"How do you do, Miss Marguerite?" The younger gentleman came forward.

"I am well, thank you," Margie said, perhaps a bit too curtly.

"Parkerson, Lawrence Parkerson. I am the son of the Thomas Parkersons. We are a banking family."

Margie nodded. She guessed she was supposed to be impressed. She wasn't. Now if he had said he was a son of some missionary overseas, she would have been.

"Perhaps you would do me the honor of sitting beside me for dinner?"

"Of course, unless my aunt has made other arrangements." —which she hoped her aunt had done.

Aunt Millicent was eyeing her every move and most likely listening to every word if she were able. Somehow she felt her aunt would oblige the young man.

When Lawrence Parkerson was called away by his father, Geri looked over at her and said, "They are priming you, Cuz. And it appears the bait is good enough for fishing tonight." Then Geri got up from the couch to search for a drink.

Margie saw Ralston watching her also as he chatted with one of the guests. Was she to be on display? She remembered his conversation with Geri earlier. Their parents wanted to dispense with her. But all she could focus on was Johnny. Will he come through with the job soon? She was of age. She could leave. But not without help.

Margie stood as Lawrence offered his arm to take her to dinner. How she wished it was a Thanksgiving dinner and all of her really true friends were there and not this crowd of worldly people.

Her aunt set her between the two men that her uncle had specifically introduced her to. Throughout the dinner they plied her back and forth with questions and invitations which she politely declined.

After dinner, Dahlia whispered to her that her room was done and she had moved all her things over. Margie wished she could escape. When the guests finally left, she went straight to her new room.

She dropped on her back on the new bed that had brought her such joy only hours before and stared at the ceiling. She thought about each of the men and all their chatter which was all about themselves. She knew more than she ever would desire to know regarding their lives and businesses and if she brought up godly things, they quieted. Clearly they could not match up to her father, Jeff, Johnny or even Doc.

A hard knock came and she sat up quickly. Aunt Millicent's normally pale cheeks were red, her mouth tight.

"Young woman, how dare you insult our guests!"

Margie shook her head slightly. "But I —"

"You have been rude to not accept their invitations, extremely rude. I'll not put up with your behavior. You shall go wherever I direct with these gentlemen."

"But we are not of like mind, Aunt Millicent."

"What does that mean? You're a fool to be religious. I won't have it. You will behave wisely or deal with the consequences."

"I am not religious. I love God. I honor him and my family."

"Well, they are dead or gone and you had better honor us as we are your family."

Tears were starting to form and Margie stiffened to keep them from cascading. When her aunt left, Margie shut the door, sat down, and quickly pulled the handkerchief out before the flood came.

The loss of her parents, missing Jeff, the heartless

family here, and the precious Thanksgiving friends faraway, were washing her face tonight.

Oh, Lord, I feel so lost. Am I to be married off to one of these egotistical men? Men who shrink at the mention of your name? I feel abandoned by everyone and left to a fate I cannot endure.

She felt the anger rising in her as she thought about her obnoxious uncle, her conniving aunt, and her mocking cousin. At least Ralston was not a real enemy.

Why don't you stop them Lord? Why do I suffer humiliation at their hands? I hate them! They are evil and cruel. I would never treat anyone like they do. I want to leave. Show me how!

She threw herself on the bed and cried her heart out. When she was finished, a still small voice spoke.

BE STILL AND KNOW THAT I AM GOD.

She heard it but she wanted to ignore it. Surely God would not make her stay, would he?

Chapter 10

A soft knock told Margie it was Dahlia, the sweet and unimposing way of this dear friend-servant.

Dahlia carried a partially wrapped gown in her arms.

Margie's face dropped. "Oh no, another dinner?"

"No, miss, more of a ball."

Margie sat down, her eyes closed in despair.

"Most ladies do enjoy balls," Dahlia said.

"Perhaps, Dahlia, but not with this crowd of people. I have no desire to touch any of these heathen men."

"I never thought of it like that. I sure don't like the gentlemen your uncle has set before you. I suppose I would be as much opposed to them as you if it were me. It's a beautiful gown though."

Then with a twinkle in her eye, Dalia said, "Perhaps you could dream of it being Johnny that you're dancing with."

Margie smiled at her. It was a pleasant thought.

How did Dahlia know what was in her heart?

Dahlia laid out the gown across the bed and they both sighed. It was an exquisite piece. Varying shades of silver and blue thread made elegant patterns throughout. Her girlish heart longed to wear it but never for these men. If only Johnny could see her in it. But would he care?

"Let's try it on, Miss."

Dahlia's brows lifted in anticipation making Margie laugh. "All right."

In no time Margie stood in front of the mirror. Her breath caught. "Oh, my."

"It's stunning, simply stunning. Perhaps you'll find a new beau at the ball."

Margie wondered if perhaps there was another man. Maybe a godly man who would take the place of these men and yet appease her uncle.

"There is nary a man who wouldn't desire to meet you, but in this dress..." Dahlia gave out a whistle.

"Thank you, Dahlia, but I have no real desire to meet anyone right now."

"Perhaps your mind is on a certain Thanksgiving guest?"

"His friendship was endearing but I shouldn't hope for such things."

"I don't know. He certainly had eyes for you."

"You were imagining it."

"I was not."

Dahlia was checking the skirt to see if any fitting needed to be done. Margie grinned at her. "Dahlia, it's your turn."

"Oh no, your aunt would have my hide."

"She's left for town. I saw her leave. Come on, help me out of it."

Amidst the "I really shouldn'ts" and the giggles, Dahlia tried on the dress.

"You look beautiful," Margie said, her hand on her heart.

"I've never put anything on like this before." Dahlia seemed in shock.

"Here." Margie ripped Dahlia's cap off and unpinned the young woman's glorious blonde hair. It fell all across her shoulders and down to her waist like a golden wrap. She was so beautiful. Margie wished she could have Dahlia go to the ball while she stayed there in her room.

A rap on the door made them both jump. Margie hurriedly stuffed Dahlia into the wardrobe.

"Yes?" Margie called at the door.

"It's me, Ralston. Have you seen Dahlia? Tell her Cook is looking for her."

"Okay, Ralston, " Margie said through the door.

They quickly put Dahlia back in order and put her cap back on.

"Thank you, Miss. What a wonderful day. It's nice to

dream once in a while."

Margie hugged her friend. "Our special secret."

"Yes, Miss Margie," Dahlia whispered.

"Dahlia, you are quite lovely you know. If you went to the ball, you would be queen."

Dahlia blushed. "Thank you, Miss." She turned to go.

"And Dahlia?"

"Yes, Miss?"

"You are a sweet friend."

"Oh, but—"

"Friend, Dahlia. You are my friend." Margie took both of her hands and held them so Dahlia would understand that she meant it.

Dahlia smiled at her as if she understood, then went on to see about Cook. But Margie called her back once more. "When is this ball?"

"In three days. At the Parkerson Mansion."

Margie closed the door and leaned against it facing the dress that now lay upon the bed. Lawrence Parkerson was the wealthy banker's son.

I do not want to do this, Lord. I want Johnny to write and tell me I have a new job and then I can pack my trunk and go far away from here, never to come back, ever.

The banker's mansion was lit up in all its glory.

"Well, isn't this the gala of the year," Geri said in her usual sarcasm, as the car approached, craning her neck at the window.

It was probably the first time Margie agreed with the obnoxious girl.

"As long as there is plenty of refreshments, Ralston will be happy," Geri continued.

"Now listen up, Ralston, you need to make a good impression or the bankers won't favor you with loans," Uncle Thornton said, his head twisting around toward the backseat. Margie wiggled uncomfortably in her new gown as the instruction continued. Her uncle chastised them often but never bothered to carry out any punishment and they knew it.

"Geraldine Louise, you shall not sit unladylike in a corner with your foolish friends and make assessments about everyone in the room."

"Yes, Father," she said, rolling her eyes.

"Marguerite." Margie jumped at her name and tightened her wrap.

Her aunt continued, "You shall dance with whomever, but Lawrence Parkerson is the host and you must favor him." Margie silently finished her aunt's sentence...because he is the banker's son.

Margie nodded slightly just as Geri let out a snort.

Her aunt whipped her head around. "Stop that, young lady!"

"That was Geri, not Margie," Ralston said.

"Well, watch your manners, anyway," her aunt said, embarrassed.

At the open doors leading to the ballroom, the Parkerson family stood greeting their guests. The stoic Lawrence stood stiffly until he saw Margie.

Her wrap had been taken by impeccably dressed servants. When her gown had been revealed, several in the area turned to stare at her. She wanted to go get her wrap and leave. But before she knew it, Mr. Parkerson grabbed her hand and pulled her in front of his wife and son.

"My dear, this lovely creature is Thornton's niece, Marguerite. The one Lawrence mentioned to you."

"How do you do, my dear?" Mrs. Parkerson assessed her hair to hem and smiled. Margie assumed it was the dress that brought the approval.

"Very well, thank you, Mrs. Parkerson. You have a lovely home."

"Excuse me, Father, Mother, I will escort Miss Marguerite to the refreshments." Margie found herself

Sandy Faye Mauck

whisked into the ballroom.

After drinking some punch, Lawrence escorted her around and talked of collections and other boring subjects. She gazed around the dance floor, uncomfortable at the men staring at them. Lawrence went to find a servant to get more refreshments.

Margie wrenched her gloved fingers together and sighed. It was the first time she was glad to see Lawrence return.

"Here, Marguerite, this is one of mother's favorite hors d'oeuvres. She is an excellent hostess. I am sure you will also be one day."

Whatever it was, it tasted horrid, but she washed it down with the punch. She smiled slightly to be polite.

A servant whisked by to retrieve their glasses and Lawrence's demeanor took on an authoritative sharpness that caused her to flinch. She wondered how he would feel about her friendship with Dahlia.

Margie began to rub her fingers together again. The tone of Lawrence's voice sliced through her sensitivities like a knife. She wished to go now, more than ever. As Lawrence walked out a little ways with the servant, two men walked closer to her. She was ready to flee. Then a hand reached for hers and she looked up to see Ralston.

"Shall we dance, cousin?"

She nodded and they took to the floor.

"The sap doesn't dance well, Margie. He'll be

stepping on your toes in no time. You looked a bit under it so I thought I'd come to save you from the frothing wolves."

"Thank you, Ralston."

"We want the same thing, you know."

"Yes?"

"To escape."

"Oh?" she said with the slightest of a nod.

"Yes, cuz, I can see it. It's written all over you. This is not the life for either of us. What became of the group you entertained for Thanksgiving?"

"I am not sure. They went back to their own lives."

"No hope of rescuing you?"

"Well, there was an offer of a job. I am waiting to hear. Please don't speak of it to anyone."

"I won't. Mum's the word."

"And you, Ralston, what are you unable to escape?"

"Father's business world. He has no tolerance of my desires, only his own."

"I'm sorry. Perhaps there is a way out for you, as well."

"I don't see it but, say I think I'll dance you over to the punch bowl and spike mine up a bit."

Margie frowned. "It won't help."

"Ah, but it does, at least until tomorrow."

"God has better ways."

"Yes? Well let's see if he gets you out of marrying

Lawrence Parkerson. Frightening thought for you—marrying that sap. He's flat as an iron."

Ralston looked into her eyes. "I hope your God delivers you." And he was off to the punch bowl.

The wolves started to gather and Margie decided it was better to dance with one than to be so conspicuous. Then there was another and another until Lawrence pulled her arm into his to go to dinner.

"I hope you are sufficiently danced now, as I lack the talent and find it abhorrent myself."

Oh good, she didn't have to dance with him. But is that the way he would treat his wife? Let her dance with all the other men and then claim her as his own when she was sufficiently "danced"?

The dining room was blinding. She'd never seen so many chandeliers in one room. The tables were filled with luxurious gilt-edged china, the crystal ware shimmering off the light, and golden table runners exuded their wealth. She was escorted to what obviously was the host table. She sighed. It was clear she was being primed for this family.

The dinner was tolerable but a richer fare than she cared for. But at least it was better than the hors d'oeuvres. The whole time her heart longed for a sumptuous Thanksgiving meal with a more charming group of people, ones she would love to be with daily. She didn't belong here with these people. She wanted to go home. But she had no home. Loneliness wrapped around her like a wall.

The chatter and indulgence carried on as Mrs. Parkerson plied her with questions.

"My dear," Mrs. Parkinson said, "are you alone except your uncle's family?"

Alone, yes she was very alone. "No, Mrs. Parkerson, I have a brother in the Philippines. He and his wife are missionaries."

"Missionaries? My heavens, dreadful occupation. I simply cannot abide their awful stories. But I suppose someone must go and straighten out the heathens."

Heathens? There? No! But here at this table. How could she be offended by wonderful missionary stories?

"Marguerite," Mrs. Parkerson said, "you have eaten very little. Is the food not to your liking?"

"Oh, no, it's quite delicious. I suppose I am caught up in the excitement of the evening." Excitement wasn't the word she was really thinking about. Distasteful might have been more honest.

"Of course, of course. Well, eat up, child. We Parkersons have strong, healthy children."

What? Did the woman truly say that? Margie was mortified and stared down at her plate, hoping no one else heard.

Lawrence patted her arm and she pulled it away from him. "Now, don't worry about Mother. She thinks

85

you're a perfect match."

Match? Her head flew up to glare straight into his beady eyes. But he was oblivious. He just smiled and she turned back to eat. After all, she wanted to be sure to have a good fat baby, didn't she? It was hard to force the food between her gritted teeth but she managed so they would ignore her and it worked.

The audacity. As if she were engaged to the obnoxious man.

Finally the meal was over and the men went for a smoke and she was at least free of Lawrence and the gawking men. But the women were snubbing her.

She saw Geri in the corner with a few of her own set. Ralston was already soused. She longed for the night to be over and be in her room visiting with Dahlia or reading letters.

"Honestly, Marguerite, you didn't look as if you were behaving pleasantly at all at the host table. We'll discuss this tomorrow," Aunt Millicent said, as Margie came through the door.

Glad for the overnight reprieve, she went quickly to her room.

"Oh, Dahlia, it was awful." Tears would normally flow, but she was too tired and too angry.

"I was afraid for you, Miss Margie."

"They practically have me married off to that man.

His mother was talking to me about children!"

"Nooo. How wretched!"

"I don't know what to do. I have nowhere to go and his mother has obviously made plans for a wedding I shall never attend."

"No, Miss, you cannot. What a horrible set of events."

Margie plopped down on the settee. "I just can't do this."

"I have an idea. Perhaps you could stay with the old doctor. Go and ask him."

"What a grand idea, Dahlia. You are so clever. But how would I get there?"

"Master Ralston."

"Yes, he favors me a little. He might do it. He saved me from dancing with Lawrence and others tonight."

"I'll go and see what I can find out about his schedule," Dahlia said.

Hope of escape laid some of Margie's anger and bitterness aside as she dressed for bed.

Oh, please make a way, Father. I have no other recourse unless you have something else in mind. And please make Ralston willing to take me to Doc's house.

She rested with hope in her heart because of the new plan but wondered if it would come to pass.

Chapter 11

Johnny threw up his hands. "I don't see how I shall endure this monstrosity of a business." Papers lay strewn over the old desk. He folded his arms as if in defiance against his uncle's horrendous lack of organization.

"It is quite a mess, sir. Perhaps a good secretary could help," Hansen said.

Johnny looked over at his secondhand man and then out the window. He stared in silence. A beautiful young secretary was waiting for his beckon and yet he couldn't hire her. There was no place for her to live. But he did suppose it was time to write her again.

"Sir?"

"Yes, yes, Hansen. I already have a secretary. She is waiting to hear from me, but she must have a decent place to live."

"I see. That does pose a problem. Perhaps there is someone she could room with. I could check around."

"Yes, please!"

After Hansen left, Johnny sat down and rested his elbows on the piled-up disaster. He bowed his head and prayed for wisdom, funds, and a place for Margie, and most of all that she was still willing to come.

He had been one minute into writing her and his thoughts chastised himself. The thoughts of Margie being stuck in that dreadful household made him angry. Such a sweet young lady badgered by her own family. He had been lax in his prayers for the situation and he needed to write her but he would wait to see if Hansen came up with anything.

His mind had wandered often to that wonderful Thanksgiving. It was a taste of pure joy and he was hungry for it to happen all over. The memory of it provided a place of solace in his loneliness and hard work. Margie made everything right. Being there at that time was perfect, excepting maybe being unconscious in the snow. He laughed to himself.

Margie gave a quick wave to Dahlia who perfectly arranged the ride to see Doc. She hoped Ralston did not find any drinks along the way and that they would be back before Aunt Millicent came home from her excursion to her sister's house.

"We're off. Glad to get away, Cuz. I begged off from Father's meeting. Nothing could make me happier."

"Thank you, Ralston, I do appreciate this." She patted the blanket on her lap, tightened her hat, and enjoyed the scenery despite the bumpy, open-air ride in Ralston's flivver.

Margie was elated to pull up to Doc's house although a bit saddle sore from the rough car.

Oh, Lord, please, please let Doc be home.

Doc was there. He saw them from the window and came right out to greet them. She introduced the men and they went inside.

"Lottie's not here, but she left some cookies. Please have some."

Lottie? Oh no, he has someone here already. Her heart sank. Her appetite diminished.

"I am so happy to see you. I have been wondering how you were getting along," Doc said.

Ralston excused himself, with a cookie in his mouth, to check on the car.

"I didn't know if it was all right to speak with the young man here. Is he one of the family? He seemed a little familiar."

"Yes, Doc, my cousin has helped me in some situations lately. I had come to see if you had a position available. But now I see," she said looking at the plate of cookies, "that you already have someone."

"Is this position for you, my dear?"

"Yes, sir, I am in a predicament."

Ralston whistled coming through the door. "Boy, is she ever! My parents have decided to marry her off to the banker's son."

"Oh, my, this does sound desperate." The doctor rubbed his chin.

"I'm sorry I've even asked. I didn't know what to do. It was Dahlia who suggested it. It never occurred to me you already had someone helping you." Margie lowered her head, embarrassed about the whole idea.

"Lottie has been helping me out, but she has already given me notice that she is getting a different position closer to home. She will be leaving next month. So you see it should work out nicely. But I can't afford to pay you much."

Margie's heart leaped. "I don't care about that. I will do everything and I eat very little."

"I can vouch for that," Ralston said.

The old man's smile turned into a wide grin. "Then I would be glad to have you."

Now Margie could sit back and enjoy a cookie. She took a bite and winced. They were awful. Well good, she wouldn't have to compete with an expert cook, anyway.

"How soon shall I come?"

"I believe she said her last day would be on the fifth. But I will make sure and send you a letter."

"Oh, thank you, Doc. I am so happy."

"Well, that's that. Shall we head back before Mother gets home?" Ralston said.

Margie was flying higher than Ralston's flivver could bounce her up and down. She couldn't wait to tell Dahlia. She would be free!

"Letter for you, boss," Hansen said.

"As if I don't have enough to sort already," Johnny said.

"Looks personal to me."

Johnny grabbed the letter from the grinning young man. "Oh, it's Margie."

"Oh?" The younger man's eyes danced with mischief.

"My new secretary."

"An old maid then?"

"Far from that," Johnny said, remembering her face like it was yesterday. The first face he saw coming out of his unconscious state. Her warm eyes melted him right off. He set the letter aside, acting busy, hoping to send Hansen on his way so he could open it. Hansen noticed and went on down to the ship. Johnny sighed and opened the envelope.

Dear Johnny,

I pray you are feeling well and are having no repercussions from your accident. I am sorry for it happening but so thankful for the holiday we enjoyed. No meal could be compared to the lovely Thanksgiving we all had together. It was a fine day, in my estimation. At least until you were made to leave.

I cannot tell you how happy I was to receive your letter. I am so looking forward to working with you in the near future and I have been anxious about your difficult project, even though the Bible tells us to be anxious for nothing.

I hope to see everyone again someday. I pray for Doc and Chipper, too. Dahlia is now my constant companion. She sends her greetings.

I look forward to the time that you are able to call for me and I can help you on a daily basis. Thank you for your consideration and friendship. I appreciate your prayers as well, for things have been rather difficult of late.

Your thankful friend,
Margie

Johnny leaned back against a dock post. I wonder what she meant by difficult? That family is difficult enough. Have they gone from bad to worse? He placed the letter in his inside coat pocket and sighed. He must bring her here soon. She saved his life, and besides that she didn't deserve to be mistreated so cruelly by her own relatives.

"Have you seen Hansen?" Johnny called to his workers.

"Over there." The men pointed to David Hansen and Johnny walked toward him.

"Have you found a place for my secretary?"

"No sir. Rose and Lydia are the only two women here and they haven't an inch to spare."

"Then we'll have to build her one."

"Really?" Hansen's eyes lit up. He was a master builder.

"Yes, it will eat up much of my personal funds, but I need to get her here." He and Hansen went back to his office. Somehow, it didn't bother him a bit to take his own funds to do something pleasant for Margie. He was already thinking how wonderful it would be to see her smiling face every day. Building a cottage for her seemed to light a new fire under him. And one Mr. David Hansen was joyfully drawing up plans.

Margie sat in her room, her mind spinning. She was

finally able to leave this place. But she had to wait almost a month. Could she continually thwart her relatives' plans? Maybe, but she would at least do her best to dissuade Lawrence Parkerson, whenever she was faced with his advances.

Ralston dropped by and gave her some brotherly advice. She wasn't sure if she should try his ideas or not. But if she got desperate, she might. If nothing else they made her giggle.

Perhaps she could dress like Geri. No, she could never do that, even in jest. The girl was perfectly scandalous.

Now let's see, if I were Lawrence Parkerson, what would I dislike intensely? He hates to dance but that won't help.

Dahlia's soft knock and entry brought joy to her heart.

"Well, tell me. I couldn't wait any longer." Dahlia's big blue eyes were wide with hope.

"The fine doctor agreed, but I must wait until the fifth of next month."

Dahlia clapped her hands.

"But Dahlia, I have to do something about Lawrence Parkerson. I need to find a way to dissuade his advances."

"Money."

"Money?"

"Yes, Miss, he's a banker's son and from what I hear a regular skinflint."

"Ah, so I must act like I want to spend all his money. Be extravagant."

Dahlia nodded with a twinkle in her eye.

The wheels were set in motion. Between Ralston's silly ideas and Dahlia's brilliant ones, Margie should have the time of her life making the banker's son abhor the day he met her.

She lay in bed that night and prayed for Jeff, wondering if her scheme was really the right thing to do. It sounded wonderful. She hoped God would agree.

Chapter 12

"Lawrence is coming to take you to show you the new library he is funding—or his father is anyway. Be presentable and pleasant or you will have our wrath to deal with."

Margie's aunt's words played in her head but today she had a new plan. She could hardly wait to see how her new scheme would play out.

The drive to the Parkerson Library wasn't far but it was enough time to start the snowball rolling.

"Lawrence, I think this is wonderful. Perhaps you could start another library in the next town or the next."

"That doesn't sound very lucrative."

"Oh, it's only money." She flipped her arm out as if she were throwing money out the car window.

"Money is very important, Marguerite."

"Of course it is. It buys all my beautiful expensive gowns and hats. And one day I shall decorate a brand-new home with expensive artifacts and paintings of well-known artists."

It was working. She had his attention and there was a delicious look of fear that had shadowed his generally stoic face. How was she to keep from laughing?

"I... I... I don't think people should be so free with their funds. Saving money is thoroughly fulfilling."

"Oh, I suppose. But it's so fun to buy things to enjoy your life. I would like to have a new car, one just for me and my outings."

"A new car? Whatever for? One car can manage a household."

"Certainly not. Especially if I should need to go to the big city and do some serious shopping." She rubbed her hands together as if anticipating such a trip.

"Serious shopping?" His face was about to make her burst out laughing. The poor man was horrified. He had more money than he knew what to do with and the thought of giving any of it up on extravagance was beyond what his poor brain could handle.

"Yes, Lawrence, the best couturiers are in the bigger cities. They use the finest imported materials and though quite expensive are absolutely tops. And, of course, if we go then we can see all the shows and concerts and make a holiday out of it."

By the time they reached the library, Lawrence was fiddling with his collar and perspiring a bit. The library matron showed them around.

"It's beautiful. I'm sure the Parkersons will be giving you much more money for books to fill the empty shelves, won't you, Lawrence?"

The poor man's jaw twitched. "I... I think we've seen enough for today. Shall we go to dinner?"

As they rode, he complained of a headache and she easily bowed out of dinner out of concern for him and he thanked her. Now what was one of those ideas Ralston had? At the last minute she decided to finish this off.

"Lawrence, would you mind terribly if we stopped? I've just been dying for something."

"Of course not."

Margie didn't mind making him wait while she went into the store. She knew he didn't really have a headache. She had become his headache.

"Lawrence, do you like gum?"

"Gum? Certainly not."

Margie took out several pieces and stuffed them in her mouth. Then she began smacking it like a wild young boy.

"Must you?"

"What?"

"The gum. It's so unladylike." His nose scrunched.

"Naw, everybody's taking to it now. It's all the fad." She quickly turned her face toward the car window, trying desperately not to smile, knowing full well if she

99

smiled she would laugh and the production would be over.

As he grimaced, she continued. "You know it's quite a nice breath cleanser. Perhaps your mother could put them out with the mints after one of her elaborate meals. What a grand idea."

He rolled her eyes and she knew she had him again. This was downright fun. She couldn't wait to tell Dahlia about it when she got home.

"No! You didn't? Not you, Miss Margie." Dahlia's mouth stood open for the longest time. Then the two of them guffawed and giggled at the joke on the miserly Mr. Lawrence.

"And I hope this finishes him off because chewing gum was awful." She rubbed her jaw.

"I don't know when I've had such a good laugh," Dahlia said.

"I only wish you could've seen his face. He was horrified at everything I said. Poor man. His miserly world would come tumbling down, married to the likes of me. But I do feel a wee bit guilty."

"As well you should. Except that the meddlers will not leave you be."

"I suppose I'm a bit justified but my conscience is still bothering me."

"And mentioning all the expenses you would incur must've made him pale."

"It was all I could do to keep from breaking out into hysterics."

Margie was beginning to feel some real remorse about her bizarre behavior the day before but she would keep it up to buy herself some time. What if he should tell his mother? Would her aunt and uncle explode if they found out? Would she be the one to speak to her aunt and the last laugh be on Margie instead of Lawrence?

It looked as if her plan didn't do a bit of good. They kept getting thrown together, yet it seemed as if Lawrence was becoming somewhat less interested.

"The thing you haven't thought of, Miss Margie, is that he is also trapped. What his parents have decided, even arranged, has been set in stone. They may not listen to anything he says," Dahlia said, as she made the bed.

"Oh, dear. I should have known. Dahlia, you're too smart to be doing this work." Margie turned from her dressing table to look at her friend.

"But it's my station in life."

"And is being married off mine?"

"No, these people are oppressing you."

"And they don't oppress you? They treat you horribly. There are times I want to just leave the table."

"I see. We're on the same sea, but carried off by different ships. "

"In this case, the same shipping company."

"Yes."

"I wish my real shipping company would send a letter soon."

"Mr. Johnny? He was a charming man. A true gentleman."

Someone was calling Dahlia's name.

"I'm being beckoned."

"A ship?"

Dahlia nodded. "Yes, and I think I need a lifeboat."

Today Margie was to meet Lawrence for lunch and face his mother again. The thought made her cringe as she stared hopelessly into the mirror.

She spent the next hour in prayer, weighted down with her deception. She finally asked for forgiveness and new thoughts came to mind.

"I don't understand, Marguerite."

"Margie."

"What?"

"Call me Margie, not Marguerite." Why did her name sound like the man had a bad cold every time he spoke it and when Johnny spoke it sounded like music?

Lawrence and Margie were driven to the hills to a very fancy home where they were to eat lunch and discuss something important with Lawrence's mother.

"But what are you trying to say, Mar-gie." He flinched at saying her more common name.

"Your parents fluffed it off didn't they? When you told them we weren't suited."

"How did you know? Who told you?"

"Never mind, Lawrence, it doesn't matter. Now listen to me. You and I both know we're not suited. God has better ideas for both our lives."

His mouth hung open as she chatted on and on all the way through the lush hills.

"But I can't do it."

"Yes, you can. Your father has no one else to leave his business to. If you are not suited to take it over then tell him."

"He'll be furious. He'll—"

"Of course, but he'll get over it because you are his son. See this is not the case for me. My family doesn't even want me. They never did. They wanted to marry me off and have some gain in it at least some social prestige, don't you see?"

Lawrence sat listening intensely having conquered his drooping jaw.

"Now Lawrence, you must decide what it is you are fully suited for and make a case for it. Talk to your father man-to-man."

"But—"

"No, you must do it. Else you should be stuck forever in a miserable situation."

Margie took a deep breath and sat deep into the seat. She had told him, giving him the encouragement he needed. Now she needed to pull out of him what his true aspirations were.

"Lawrence, tell me. What have you always wanted to do when you became a man?"

"You will laugh."

"I certainly will not." She thought if she could keep from laughing at her deception, she certainly could keep from laughing now.

"I wanted to be an architect. To plan and build businesses and homes."

"Splendid. Why would anyone laugh at that? What fun you would have. Surely your father would approve. You can even plan his bank expansions."

The wheels in Margie's head spun wildly.

"And banking?" Margie asked.

"I deplore it."

"Then you must fight for this. Where can you learn to be an architect?"

"They offer it many places. I checked into it once or twice. My uncle is an architect, as well."

"But you got discouraged."

"Yes, Mar-gie, my apologies, I was used to Marguerite. But I do feel encouraged now."

"Good. But you must plan this perfectly. Show him your skills and ideas. Can you work with your uncle?"

He nodded. Then the mansion came into view so Margie and Lawrence quickly made a pact to curtail the relationship. She even gave him a hint to where she was going next month. It was truly fun to have a friend of her forced relationship. And it freed them both to go with their hearts' desires.

They survived the luncheon, thanks to other interesting guests that took over Lawrence's mother. She and Lawrence looked more like lovers than they ever did before, laughing and chatting. She felt as if she had released the door of a prisoner and was on her way out herself.

When Dahlia came to say goodnight, Margie told her of her day and Lawrence's plight.

"Miss Margie, I cannot even think of how you managed such a wonderful thing."

"I take no credit. It was truly the voice and vision of God that led me. And I feel free already. Poor Lawrence. He'd have been married to not only a job he hated but a woman who would've made him miserable."

"Not you miss. You would've plucked up and done all right by him. Though you wouldn't have been happy."

"Well, we're friends now. It's quite amazing really." Margie turned to Dahlia as she pulled the pins out of her hair. "I am truly excited for him."

"But what of your uncle? Won't he put another match in your face?"

"No, for I must stand up and tell him I have a position. I am of age."

"Keeping the doctor's house? A maid like me. Oh, Miss." Dahlia's head dropped and Margie stood and grabbed hold of her shoulders.

"There is nothing wrong with being a maid. If I should marry and have no servants, will I not keep my own home?"

Dahlia nodded. "But it is a position for the likes of me, not you."

"We are really no different. I am also at the mercy of my uncle am I not?"

"Yes, until you leave. Oh, Miss, I will have no one

again when you are gone." A tear slipped down the maid's cheek and Margie held her close. They both seemed destined to fight loneliness.

"I will find some way to send for you. God will make a way. I know he will."

"Yes, Miss."

"Now, finally you can call me Margie and not get in trouble for it."

"Margie. Yes, Miss." The two laughed at her misstep.

Chapter 13

Every day Margie hoped for a letter from Johnny or Doc. It didn't seem like them not to write. Concerned, she prayed more for them. Perhaps they were ill or there was some great problem. The thought also came to mind that Johnny had sent for his beloved and had forgotten all about her.

Dahlia came through the door, her face blazing. "The audacity!"

"What is it, Dahlia?"

"I found this letter on your aunt's bureau."

"Dahlia, calm down. God showed it to you and I have it, so let's see what it is all about."

Dahlia sat with Margie on the settee, trying to catch her breath while Margie read it.

"It's from Johnny. He could not find a place for me so he decided to build me one." They smiled at each other with childlike delight.

"He said it shouldn't be too long before it's ready."

Margie looked up again grinning as Dahlia clasped her hands together.

Margie stood up and tossed the letter to her friend. "Read it. I could dance for joy!" She stopped suddenly. "We must thank God for this."

"I don't know how to properly thank God."

"Have you never thanked him?" Margie stared at her friend, taken aback.

"Yes, but not proper like, beautiful words and prose."

Margie shook her head. "Dahlia, God doesn't care about prose or fancy words. He cares about you and your soul's condition. Think of him as a kind father."

Dahlia's big blue eyes looked into hers. "My father was unkind."

"Then I shall tell you about mine. He was wonderful. I so wish he were here. It's sad but I have heard the people get their ideas about God from their earthly fathers. If you think your father was cruel and harsh, you might think your heavenly Father is also cruel and harsh. My sister-in-law, Adele, Jeff's wife, was abandoned by her father. She had a time of it believing that God would never abandon her." The two friends chatted about Margie's father and how wonderful he was, yet even he could not compare to the incredible love of their heavenly Father.

Dahlia popped up. "Oh, I must get to work."

"Can I help you?"

"No, you stay here and enjoy your letter."

Father, is there a way out of this awful place for Dahlia? How can I help her?

IT'S ALL IN MY HANDS.

Oh, Father, I am so glad for this letter. And for Doc to take me on. How will I keep my aunt and uncle happy until then?

The thought came to mind straight from the Holy Spirit. She must see Lawrence!

"Really? Is that what you want, Margie?"

"Yes, Lawrence. I think this is my way to keep my uncle and aunt contented until I'm able to leave."

"Yes, it makes sense, to keep seeing each other, but won't people talk more about us? I mean…"

"Yes, I suppose and we must find a good way to end it."

"I must say, I don't mind spending time with you, Margie. You have been a good friend." Lawrence smiled and patted her hand, reminding her of his patronizing behavior, which made her happy she would not be marrying him. But he had become a friend and she was glad of it.

They spent their outings talking of his architectural endeavors and how to approach his father. It was work to put the fire under him but the more his heart spoke of the work, the more determination and courage grew in him.

Two weeks passed swiftly under the new plan and Margie knew she must write to Doc for she had heard nothing from him. Could that letter also be stolen from the post? If her aunt read it, how would Margie respond to her accusations?

She sat to write to Doc just as Dahlia entered the room.

Dahlia shut the door and turned to Margie with big eyes and a letter in her hand.

"You must hurry with this one, she's coming back soon and to miss letters twice would not bode well."

Margie took the letter quickly, gently opening it she sped through the contents. At a noise in the yard, Dahlia hurried to the window. "She's back. What do we do?"

"Take it back and pray she gets busy and waylaid from reading it."

She took it from Margie, sealed it up, and hurried out.

Margie was trying to remember every detail of the letter that was not very detailed. It spoke of the position being available earlier if she desired. Was it the twenty-second of this month? She wasn't sure.

She was praying and looking out the window to the front yard below, remembering the day Johnny came into her life. The rescue and Johnny's eyes opening just as she touched his cheek.

Her daydream dissolved as the door flew open and Dahlia rushed in. "She's asked for you and has the letter in her hand."

Margie froze, trying to think and pray.

FOR THE HOLY GHOST SHALL TEACH YOU IN THE SAME HOUR WHAT YE OUGHT TO SAY.

She patted Dahlia's arm. "It will be all right. God will tell me what to do."

But Dahlia did not look convinced.

"Pray for me."

Dahlia nodded.

"What is the meaning of this letter?" Aunt Millicent flapped the letter in Margie's face.

It occurred to Margie she was not supposed to know about this letter.

"What do you mean?"

She shoved the letter into Margie's hand and she read it slowly, praying as she went. She looked up at her aunt's pinched face.

"Well?"

"Um, it's a position. Do you always read my mail?"

"Who is the position for? You?"

Suddenly the words came out as if not her own. "No. It's for Dahlia."

"Dahlia? The maid?"

Why must she say her name like it was offensive?

"Yes, I heard of the opening from a friend and wondered if Dahlia might not be suited to it."

"She's our maid. Why would you do such a thing?"

"It appears you don't care for her."

"Well, she's not the best but…"

"It was an urgent position and I thought of her."

"You thought. You thought. You think too much for a young woman."

Margie bit her lip, praying for wisdom.

"Well, then! If she wants a new position then so be it. But she'll get no letter from me as to her service. Tell her to come if you see her upstairs."

"Yes, ma'am."

"You what?" Dahlia stood gaping.

"I told her it was for you," Margie said.

Dahlia was stupefied. "But it's your position."

Margie smiled sheepishly. "No, it's yours. God told me what to say."

"But if I go, what will you do?"

"Wait until Johnny calls for me."

"But—"

"Now go and face my aunt and say little. You'll be dismissed rudely, I imagine, but God will make a way. You may have to go to Doc's early and see if he'll take you with no wages."

"I have some money set back. I can board for a week or so."

"Wonderful. God gave me the words. That I am sure of. I had no idea I would say what I did. Haven't I prayed for an escape for you?"

"Yes, but not at your expense." Dahlia's lips quivered.

"Dear friend, being with the doctor will be such a blessing. God knows what he's doing." Margie kissed her cheek and gently shoved her on her way.

Dahlia sighed and lingered at the door.

"Dahlia, God's ways are not always our ways, but he orders our steps. And remember, he is a good and loving father."

Dahlia nodded and left. Margie sat on her bed. Oh,

what a turn of events. She was mulling over her conversation when Ralston knocked his typical knock at her door.

"Come in, Ralston."

"What's going on, Margie? Mother's in a tizzy and the servants are all chattering. Something about a letter you received."

"Humph, a letter *I* received? It was addressed to me but your mother has decided to filter my mail."

"Really? I must remember that. What did the letter say?"

"It was from the kind doctor."

His brows raised. "Uh oh. Does she know?"

"Only that Dahlia will be taking the position I found for her."

His eyes narrowed, his head cocked. "But…"

She put up her hand. "I know. It was mine but this is how it all came together now, so don't mention it please. I will figure out how to make things work for myself. God will help me."

"He didn't help much this time." Ralston's sarcasm made her cringe.

"Oh, but he did. Dahlia is free. You and I come next, Ralston."

"That's a better way to look at it I suppose."

"Tell me, Ralston, what is your dream?"

"To build things like bridges or ships."

"All right. Go and think on it. Tonight at dinner you will share it and I will support you."

"I don't know." He shrugged his shoulders.

"Uncle Thornton will not approve?"

"I don't know, I never asked him."

"You never…" Margie rolled her eyes.

"No." Ralston stood tall and lanky and yet looked like a whipped pup.

"It is high time then. See you at dinner."

"It won't work."

"You must try, but act enthusiastic."

She ushered him out and noted the slight lift to his stature as he left.

Oh, Father, must I push every bird out of their nest while I just sit here?

The enemy came in like a flood and the loneliness overtook her like a black cloud as she sat looking at the person in the mirror. Am I to marry Lawrence after all? The thought horrified her.

It didn't take long before she could hear Jeffrey's voice calling her Pocahontas and her father telling her she was much more special than even a little sparrow, a plain boring little sparrow who has fallen to the ground. She could hear her mother's voice saying that God will make a way and to never give up hope. She didn't think much about those words back then, but today they seemed to be pouring life into her.

I'll not worry about myself for you will take care of me. I'll set myself to pray for Dahlia, Doc, Chipper, Lawrence, Johnny, and of course this household.

She prayed in all diligence until Dahlia's gentle rap came and brought her out of the heavenlies and back to this world.

"Time for dinner, Miss Margie."

"How did it go?"

"Just as you said. I am dismissed. I have a few days."

Margie nodded. "You will be blessed at Doc's house."

Margie hurried to tidy her hair and go out the door with her friend.

"The whole time she was dismissing me, I wanted to laugh. Not having to listen to this contentious family will be peace enough."

"Don't I know it."

"I hate leaving you to them."

Dahlia was cut off with the frustrated cook downstairs hollering for her, and she hurried off.

Margie hurried too because she had promised Ralston to stand with him tonight. They didn't much care about what she had to say about anything, but she would try.

The family sat as if waiting for her but she remembered Geri was always late, loving to make an entrance.

"Why can't she manage to make it to dinner on time?" her uncle said, in his normal growling tone. He never once sounded like her father whose voice was pure kindness and even when he was angry, his tone was only stern.

"I told you before. She has gone to the mountains with her friends," her aunt said.

Good. Ralston had a better chance without Geri's ridicule.

About the midpoint of dinner, Ralston looked at Margie. She gave him a nudging nod to proceed and he did. It was an amazing thing. When Ralston poured out his desires, her uncle stopped eating and listened intently.

Ralston finished and her uncle was thoughtful. When his aunt was about to start chattering, he told her to be quiet. The look on her face was so funny, Margie had to cover her smile with her napkin.

"If you go to school to learn these things, will you stop drinking?" her uncle asked, his face like stone.

Ralston looked at him shocked and then to Margie, then back to his father again. "Yes! Absolutely," he said.

Ralston was ready to explode with excitement and Margie was in heaven. A double blessing.

Thank you, Father!

The sun was barely thinking about breaking the horizon when Margie woke. She had dreamt she was reading one of Jeff's letters, so she went to her drawer and pulled them out. One fluttered to the floor. She sat the others aside and opened that one.

> *My Dear Little Sister,*
>
> *I pray you are well and happy so far from us. Every time I asked the Lord if I should bring you here, it is a decided no. You have a different work to do for God.*
>
> *I know what you are going through is not easy, but be brave, little Pocahontas, and remember God has a plan in all of it.*

She dropped the letter to her lap. She was beginning to see some of the plan. There was the Thanksgiving with Johnny and the others. Dahlia and Doc needed each other. She needed to pray for Chipper to be adopted and for Johnny's business. And now Ralston, which made her smile.

But now what? The thought of being left with her aunt and uncle and Geri and the younger girls when they came back from school was distressing. But she did something she was taught to do from a young age:

bringing into captivity every thought to the obedience of Christ. So she must not dwell on her condition, but thank God in all things.

She pulled the letter from her lap and continued to read.

I know God has a very special place for you to be and you will not be lonely for he sets the lonely in families.

He sets the lonely in families. The scripture Johnny mentioned. But Jeff, this is not a family. They detest me. Which would be worse staying here or marrying Lawrence? One horrid family to another. She was going to be taking thoughts captive all day.

She read on.

Obey his Holy Spirit, sister girl. Don't be afraid to step out into new places.

New places?

Remember James 3:17 says that the wisdom of God is peaceable and easy to be entreated...

Yes, my dear brother, I'm encouraged. Even hard things are easier when God gives you that peace that comes with his wisdom. I have no peace, but perhaps other doors will open and I will feel that peace.

She held her dear brother's letter to her heart and the tears flowed. The only loving family she had left was far away. But she would be thankful for their letters. She would be content. It was time to write and tell them all her amazing tales.

"Mr. Lawrence has arrived, Miss Margie."

"Thank you, Dahlia. Will you post this letter to Jeff for me, please?"

"Of course. I don't know if I can bear to escape and leave you here."

"Nonsense. God has a plan, my dearest friend. Perhaps Ralston will bring me for a visit." She reached her reassuring hand for Dahlia's and squeezed it.

Lawrence waited for her in the parlor.

"I have news. Will you come for a drive?"

"Certainly." It wasn't often the stoic man was animated. He must have interesting news.

"I'll get your wraps, Miss," Dahlia said.

The drive was beautiful. The snowcapped mountains were set like a painting against the yellow greens of the trees. The air was still cool but the harsh winter chill was running off to make way for spring. They got out and stood on an overview looking over a valley. The air was clear and refreshing. She took a deep breath.

"It's a lovely place, Lawrence. But you said you had news."

"Yes, Margie. My father has been won over."

"Yes?" She clapped her gloved hands together and quietly thanked God.

"It was just as you said. He thought it was a wonderful idea. I think his brain was calculating all the savings of not paying out so much to build more banks." He laughed heartily and it did her heart good to hear it.

"I cannot tell you how happy that makes me, Lawrence."

His countenance changed slightly. "Margie, we're great friends now. Would you not consider our previous arrangement?"

Fear came over her like a dark cloud. The haunting fear that she was supposed to marry him. There was no peace in that thought. She should have some sort of peace, right?

"Oh, Lawrence, I'm flattered but—"

"We're more suitable, don't you think?"

Margie sighed. Her tongue was tied. "In some ways..."

"Don't say no yet. Please think on it for a time."

"All right, Lawrence, I will pray. But I am elated over you having your father's blessing."

"Thank you. I wanted to share it with you first. If it hadn't been for you…"

"I only encouraged you to do what was in your heart already, Lawrence. Rest assured God has done the miracle."

"Yes, I believe you are right and I shall thank him at church tomorrow."

"You don't have to attend church to thank him, Lawrence. You can thank him right here and now in his glorious creation." She reached out her arm to the snowcapped mountains.

"Yes, I suppose I can, can't I? But is it proper?"

She rolled her eyes but he didn't see. "If you were God, and you created all these beautiful, wonderful things for man, would you want your children to come and thank you in a house built by men or in the creation that you made for them?"

"I never thought of it that way. It makes perfect sense."

Margie smiled and looked out across the valley, waiting for Lawrence to pray. When he did, her heart rejoiced.

A breeze came up and they opted to go back, both quiet and peaceful. She hoped her true peace would come in not agreeing to marry Lawrence.

Chapter 14

"Do you think you might marry Lawrence?" Dahlia's blue eyes reflected a bit of horror, making Margie giggle.

"No, of course not. He isn't truly interested. He is just caught up in all my encouragement."

"Yes, I found that to be intoxicating myself," Dahlia said, smiling.

"Are you all packed?"

"Yes, I haven't much really."

"Hmm…" Margie opened her wardrobe. Her own things were fairly plain but she did have the blue silk Margie gave Dahlia to wear on Thanksgiving. And another skirt and blouse that would suit Dahlia and her lovely complexion.

She pulled them out. "Here, try this on. I know the blue silk fits you but this might not."

"Haven't you done enough for me? They are yours."

"Yes, they are mine and not Aunt Millicent's, so I am free to give them as I desire. It will be my going-away gift to you. If only I could give you some of the nicer gowns but I feel as though they're not mine."

"But you'll need these if Johnny calls for you."

Margie shook her head. "No, I will be fine. I think I will make something myself in the evenings when I have no dear friend to visit with."

"You make me sad to leave you, Miss."

"I do hope someday you will call me Margie."

"Perhaps, if I write it over and over in letters. I'll send my letters through Benson, so your aunt doesn't steal your letters."

"Good idea. She wouldn't think to look among the gardener's posts. Perhaps I should give his name to Jeff and Johnny."

Dahlia tried on the clothing and they fit.

"These are the nicest I've ever had."

"You'll have something for church and socials."

It was hard to part but Margie promised to ask Ralston to take her to Doc's for a visit and that seemed to smooth it over.

"Hansen!"

"Yes, sir?"

"I need you to find someone to supervise the house

finishing because you are going on a trip, " Johnny said.

The eager young man's face made Johnny smile. He was given his instructions and would be off to find a certain charming secretary and help her travel.

Johnny wanted to make the trip himself but it was foolish to leave. There was no one who could take his place. He hoped his letter would give her peace traveling with Hansen. He also hoped Hansen would not talk her ears off the entire trip. By the time she arrived the finishing touches on her cottage would be done, and she would not be subject to those wretched people who dared to call her family any longer. That alone made his heart happy.

He gazed out toward the sea. Would she love it like he did? It had taken him by surprise. The company was running now but still somewhat shaky and she knew this. He told her. He was remembering her and it made him so excited to have her here and show her his new venture and the magnificent sea that God had brought him to.

Was he doing this to pay her back for saving his very life? He supposed so but there was more. He didn't want to leave her that day to that heartless aunt and uncle. He hoped she was still there and would come. But there was yet more in his heart. He missed her. In fact he missed the whole Thanksgiving group. There was Doc, Chipper, and Dahlia. Then there was Margie. He sighed. The longing was deeper than he realized. He thought of her every day whenever there was a free moment.

He stayed in contact with Doc and Chipper. They had won his heart. He wished he could do something for Chipper, to get him out of that awful place and that bully of a headmaster. As he promised, he told the boy about the sea and the ships. He sent him a Bible and shared godly wisdom with him for his trials. Oh, how the boy would love it here. He would be fishing, playing in the tide pools, searching for whales and otters, and playing captain on the ships. Those were things a young boy should be doing—not working for evil men.

And Doc, wouldn't he love to sit and watch the sunset over the sea. He would get him a rocking chair and a captain's hat. He could help with minimal health issues on the dock.

Johnny took a deep breath of sea air and went back into the reality of the worst mess of an office he'd ever seen. He hoped Margie wouldn't take one look at it and want to go back. It was awful to have her come and face it but he hadn't had a chance to touch it himself.

Margie waved as Dahlia went on her way to Doc's and did her best to hold back her tears. And it was a good thing because Lawrence showed up right after.

"I have a surprise."

"Oh," she said, wishing she could go up to her room and sulk instead.

Afraid to face the engagement answer, Margie tried to put him off, but he wouldn't budge.

They drove toward his home, then veered off to the east. When they stopped, he reached for her hand and led her to nothing.

"It's mine."

"What's yours?"

"This property," he said, waving his arms in full spread.

"That's nice. It seems a lovely spot. But what will you do with it?"

"I would build a house and an amazing office for myself. Father gave it to me. He said he could call it a wedding gift." There was a rare twinkle in his eye.

Margie's jaw dropped and she stared out across the property. She started calculating. She would be married to Lawrence, living here, next to his parents. She shook her head. This couldn't be God's will, could it? Would marrying Lawrence be better than being lonely in the house of her uncle?

"I know you haven't decided but wouldn't it be a wonderful place? Can you see it?"

See it, yes, but not for her. Not at all.

She couldn't answer him. Something constricted her throat. When she finally spoke, she asked if he'd mind taking her home. She wasn't feeling well. It was true for her stomach was turning for lack of food, the emotional distress of Dahlia's departure, and now this. She needed to pray. She needed answers.

If only Jeff's letter had come. The one where she asked his advice about marriage.

Lawrence left a bit melancholy, even though she tried to explain that she wasn't feeling well before their excursion.

Margie ran quickly up to her room and shut the door just as the tears begin to spill. She fell to her knees and wept, trying hard to speak but nothing came out. She pulled herself up and lay across the bed feeling numb. A breeze blew in the window floating something off the bureau. She got up to shut the window and looked down to see a new letter from Jeff.

Dearest Margie,

I hope you are well. We pray for you daily and miss your sweet smile. Jeff felt I should answer your letter. He felt you needed a feminine point of view.

You asked if you should ever marry someone you don't have strong feelings for. I will say this much, you must never marry because you think it is the only way out of a hard situation. That would be unwise. You must take it to the Lord and ask him to make all things clear. I, personally, would never marry someone who did not seem quite right or who does not believe as I do. You will spend many hard times in a marriage and you need a special relationship to survive and be strong. Trust God and wait for his clear direction. The thought of marrying a man should never make you feel fearful or apprehensive but should incite joy. And in prayer it should be confirmed of God by his word, his spirit, and his peace. Remember the Bible says we are not to be unequally yoked.

Sometimes when you have several choices before you, you think you must choose one of them but God may have another altogether.

Her dear sister-in-law went on to remind her about Margie's own lovely parents. She walked to the window and saw them in the eye of the past, laughing, holding each other, and smiling sweetly. She wanted nothing less than that. Then she tried to think of how a marriage with Lawrence would be but all she could see was Johnny's face. Did he have to come into her life and spoil it? No, he didn't spoil it. He was a blessing. No one comes close to the kind, handsome man in any way, but she feared his heart was taken.

She turned as a rap at the door made her jump. She hoped she didn't look like she cried her heart out.

"Dinner, Miss Marguerite," the new maid said, through the door.

Oh, how she missed Dahlia.

As she went downstairs she felt Geri almost at her heels.

"Ah, here comes the soon-to-be married niece," Aunt Millicent said, pleased with herself.

Ralston looked up surprised and Geri laughed behind her. Anger rose in her. She had just about had enough.

"I am not soon to be married. I have no engagement," Margie said as nicely as the words of her frustration would allow.

"It's fairly obvious as long as you don't string him along too long." Her aunt snapped at her like a grouchy old dog and she felt like growling right back, but she held her tongue.

She ate and excused herself to get some air. Back in her room she buried herself in making a new dress, one she hoped to wear as a secretary.

She didn't want to live with this family and she did not want to marry Lawrence but what else was there? Then Adele's words from her letter reminded her she didn't just have two choices. But she felt bound, stuck in the mire, with no way of escape.

Hypocrite! The enemy shouted in her ear and she accepted his assessment. She was faithless. But then something rose in her spirit. No! I will not listen. My God will help me. He is my rock and my deliverer and in him only do I trust.

She decided to sneak down and get some tea and as she walked by Geri's room, she heard the arguing.

"She's a perfect little fool. Mother's fed up with her." Geri's scratchy voice came barreling out into the hall.

"No, she isn't," Ralston said. "She has a right to marry who she likes."

"She'd be set for life with Lawrence Parkerson. She could live her own life and ignore him."

"Being set for life is not everything my bohemian sister."

She didn't want to hear anymore. Even tea wouldn't make her feel better. She was a little thankful for Ralston, but still beaten down.

What do I do, Father? Why hasn't Johnny written? Am I hoping for things I cannot have?

Chapter 15

"Johnny sent you? Oh, I'm so glad! Please, come in."
Dahlia thought she would burst with joy. She hoped he
had a message that would include the job for Margie.

"I only stopped by to see how Doc was doing.
Johnny wanted a report and to wish him well."

"We are fine here, young man," Doc said.

"Hansen, sir, David Hansen." He reached for Doc's
hand.

"Come, you must be hungry, Mr. Hansen. I'll fix you
something to eat," Dahlia said.

"Thank you, Ma'am. That sounds great."

"Dahlia is my lovely helper and friend, David. You
chose well to stop here and eat."

Doc was making her blush. She knew it, she always
knew. That rosy skin of hers just bursts like the sunrise.
Ugh! And the man is staring.

"Johnny knows Dahlia, too, David. But she just came
to help me recently, so he didn't know she was living

here." He refused to call her his maid. It was silly, of course, but sweet. She was so at peace with Doc. He cared for her like a gentle father.

"I see. Then I will tell him when I go back."

"Certainly you didn't just come to see how I was," Doc said.

"No, sir. I have come to retrieve my boss's new secretary."

Doc and Dahlia smiled at each other and she thought she would jump for joy. God has come through for Margie. Nothing could make her happier.

Dahlia finished the meal she had started earlier and the three of them sat and chatted. David had insisted she call him David and he smiled constantly. But it was a heartwarming smile with his charming way and handsome face. His hair was almost the same color as hers. She thought his eyes were also blue, but she couldn't look long enough to be sure because he was always looking her way.

Something was up with Doc. He was scheming. Then it came.

"David, do you know the way to Margie's?"

"I have my map, but I have never been in the area before." He pulled his map out of his pocket to show them.

"I don't think you will find her with this. It is a bit tricky, son," Doc said. "I think Dahlia needs to go with you."

Dahlia bit her bottom lip, thinking about the scene that might unfold at the house. But she would love to be there when her cherished friend left that awful family of hers and they could visit all the way home before she left for her new job.

"Does Miss Margie know you are coming?"

"I don't know. Mr. Johnny said she doesn't always get her letters. But I have a letter of introduction from him."

"Oh, yes, I know very well she does not get her letters. You won't need that letter if I go with you. We are best of friends."

"It will be nice to have someone to talk to beside myself. I am a very boring man, I think."

They all had a laugh and after eating, the two went on their way.

Dahlia and David chatted like magpies traveling to retrieve Margie. They had much in common and agreed on a great many things. Then they started to get close to the house.

"What is it, Dahlia? You seem nervous."

"I am. I just left this awful place to work for Doc and they are none too happy with me. Maybe you could go in alone and when you see her, whisper to her I am here."

"Very well."

He returned quickly. She hoped Margie wasn't off getting married or something.

"No one answered," David said.

"I will check with the gardener. He will know."

She came back solemn.

"Dahlia, is everything all right?"

"She's gone. He said she left a note and didn't say where she was going. She took her trunk." Then she broke down.

"We'll find her. Don't cry. Did he mention when she left?"

"Today, after noon."

"Which way would she go?"

"Surely the way we came. But she could be walking on footpaths and we missed her."

"Let's go before we run out of daylight."

They got into the car and raced back to the main road.

Tears kept blurring Dahlia's eyes but she searched intently along the road.

"Why would she leave, Dahlia"

"It is a long story but I will share it as we go."

Margie sat wondering why on earth she left, except her temper flared. Another misstep, she supposed. But it was getting dark and she hadn't made it nearly as far as she thought she could.

"Margie! Margie!"

Was she hearing things in her exhaustion? It sure sounded like Dahlia. But it couldn't be Dahlia, she's at Doc's.

"Mar-geee, it's Dahliaaa!"

It *is* Dahlia! And there she was in a blue car with some man driving slowly. She ran frantically waving. "I'm here, Dahlia."

"Stop. There she is." Dahlia jumped out. She ran and enveloped her friend in her arms. David retrieved her trunk and they hurried on their way.

The two of them sat in the back seat.

"Oh, Miss Margie, I was so frightened."

"Oh, Dahlia, don't call me Miss Margie. I don't know who I am but a fool. They made me so angry, I couldn't take one more day."

"Margie, this is David Hansen. He was sent by Johnny to take you to your new job."

"What?"

"You have your secretary job and a place to live," Dahlia said, taking Margie's face in her hands to stop the confusion.

"Oh!" She felt like a little spoiled child that needed a

spanking but was given a trip to the sweet shop instead. Their excitement made the trip go quickly.

"I hope you don't mind, but I shared your plight with David," Dahlia said.

"No, I don't mind. David, is Johnny ready for me to work now?"

"I should say. He has the business running fairly well but that office, oh boy!" He whistled.

"I have a place to stay?"

"You sure do. I saw to the whole scheme myself. A charming sea cottage just for you. Nicest place in the area."

Margie and Dahlia looked at each other and squealed just the slightest squeal of delight. After all, they couldn't act like schoolgirls in front of him.

"You sound happy back there," David said.

"Oh, you just drive," Dahlia teased back, red as an apple.

Margie looked at each of them. They seemed to already have a connection. She grinned at Dahlia and she started to blush.

"Never you mind my blushing. I know that look."

But Margie just smiled a knowing smile.

As they drove up to Doc's, he greeted them at the door.

"I have another surprise," Doc said.

Then he moved to the side and there was Chipper.

"Chipper!" the women shouted in unison.

The lad was enveloped in hugs and kisses until Doc saved him by telling them all to come in. "It's getting too cold."

"Just like Doc, always thinking about health." Dahlia winked at Doc.

Obviously, Doc and Dahlia were getting on well in the new situation. It made Margie happy. But everything was making Margie happy.

"Oh, Chipper, I have missed you so. I hope we didn't overdo our hugs and kisses. Are you well?" Margie asked.

"Yes, Ma'am. I manage. I haven't been hugged like that since my ma died."

Doc interrupted by explaining about the arrangements for sleeping.

"Chipper can stay?" Margie asked.

"Yes, I have him once a month. I, uh, pay him to fish and such," Doc said, making them all laugh.

Dahlia and Margie chatted in Dahlia's room until they couldn't keep one eye open.

Chapter 16

A loud knock at the door set the barely waking household into a stir. Dahlia and Margie peeked out their door to see.

"Hello, anyone home?"

David rose from the floor. "I know that voice!"

He opened the door and let Johnny in.

"Hello Boss. What are you doing here?"

Margie looked at Dahlia, they mouthed "Johnny" Then they quickly shut the door and started dressing and fixing their hair. It seemed there were two young men to impress today.

Dahlia went out first. "It is you, Mr. Johnny. I am so glad."

"Yes, it appears we have a reunion going on," he said.

Margie watched him. He was much more handsome than she remembered.

He looked up and saw her. There was a moment, a

sweet moment of connection. She didn't understand it but she could hardly breathe.

"Miss Margie, you are here. They retrieved you already?"

She nodded and then he was there, standing before her, face-to-face, grinning at her.

"I cannot believe you did such a wonderful thing for me, in building a cottage."

"I built the cottage," David said, waving his arm from the other side of the room.

"He did," Johnny said, "at my bidding. I only hope it will suit you."

"I am sure it will. But why did you come if you sent David for me?"

"He didn't trust me," David said in jest.

"That's not true, Hansen. I felt like I should have been the one to come. It wasn't proper for me to send a stranger in my stead." He turned to face her again. "I apologize, Miss Margie."

Margie sighed. "My dear friend, you could have sent an elephant and I would be on it."

That laughter finally woke the last sleeper.

"Huh?" Chipper rubbed his eyes. "Is this a dream? Is that you, Mr. Johnny?"

Johnny laughed, that deep loving laugh like Margie's father. "It is me, not a dream, lad."

The boy ran for him and Johnny lifted him into a

bear hug.

"I hope you didn't mind a hug," Johnny said.

"It was better than all the smooches from the ladies," Chipper whispered.

"That sounds good. I don't believe I had the pleasure of such a greeting." Johnny looked around knowing full well they all heard Chipper. Margie gave him a sly smile.

A bark from outside caused Chipper to run for the door. "It's Coll!"

The group enjoyed ham and flapjacks, potatoes and preserves as they told many of the things that had transpired in their lives.

"I hope you still want me for a secretary. I have been such a fool, running off."

"Of course, I want you," Johnny said. "Please don't go back now."

"I would never go back, even if you didn't want me."

"I wish I could work for you," Chipper said as he tossed little pieces of the ham to the dog.

"We will help somehow. You must pray, Chipper, like I taught in the letters."

"Yessir. I have been, just like you said."

"Unless Chipper would get adopted," Doc said.

"Naw, no one ever adopts anyone my age unless it is a cute girl or a brawny fella. I will be off to the salt mines soon."

"Salt mines?" Dahlia watched for an explanation.

"It is an expression. Hard work. In his case the factories," Doc said.

The room got quiet. Then Margie got up and helped Dahlia with the dishes.

"Enough—go and visit. I'll be there in a minute," Dahlia said, nodding her to the dining room.

As she went back into the dining room, she noticed David Hansen taking some things into the kitchen. Her mind spun a little romance that made her smile.

"Chipper, did your little friend get adopted?" Margie asked.

"Yes, Ma'am, and I miss him. I feel real alone now."

Margie looked at the group that had gathered together in such a strange way. There was not one that didn't understand what that loneliness felt like for Dahlia had said even David was also without family.

"But, I am glad for Doug. They looked like nice people. I read their letters to him as he couldn't read, yet. His new folks wanted a son not a slave. He told me they wanted him to go to school at the little schoolhouse in their town. Doug said their son died and they wanted a boy like him."

Margie couldn't speak. If she did she'd make a blubbering fool out of herself. One more family broken by the fever and the joy of restoration of their lonely broken hearts. Her heart was fraught with emotions.

"You are a brave lad, Chipper. I am sure he will always remember you for protecting him and being a friend," Doc said.

Margie excused herself and had a good quick little cry in Dahlia's room. When she returned, Johnny was having David pack up the cars.

"I don't know when I've had so much fun," Hansen said, calling Coll into his car.

"I agree, but I have never seen you so quiet, Hansen," Johnny pointed with his eyes toward Dahlia. Hansen raised his brows and sighed. Yes, it was just as he suspected. Hansen may be a bit happier about getting the mail after this.

Margie was clinging to Dahlia as he walked back toward the group.

"Don't forget my promise," Margie said.

"I won't. I am so happy for you." Dahlia kept wiping tears with her handkerchief and Johnny felt it best to leave them be. He wondered what Margie had promised.

It was hard to say goodbye. Doc had Dahlia now, so that was easier but Chipper, his little fellow, troubled him. He had to find a way to help Chipper and soon.

144

"So do you think I fit in to this great Thanksgiving family?" Hansen asked, almost with a little melancholy.

"Well, we seem to all be without family. Is that the way it is for you too, son?" Doc asked.

"Yes, it is, Doc. I have been on my own since I was a little older than Chipper. My father died in the war and my mother's heart gave out. I have a brother somewhere but I have yet to find him."

"I would say that more than qualifies you, David. But we would have let you be a part on any account."

"Thanks, Doc." Doc grasped Hansen's hand and exchanged some small talk.

As he and Margie said their goodbyes to Doc and Chipper, Dahlia and Hansen said an exceptionally long goodbye. Johnny watched out of the corner of his eye and wondered.

Chapter 17

"I think it was a good thing Coll was along. She will keep David from a long boring trip. But I know I won't be bored one little bit," Johnny said.

"It was wonderful being altogether again," Margie said, settling in for the long ride.

"It was. It was the best thing that happened since Thanksgiving."

"For me, too."

"David told me about the cottage you had him build for me. I am humbled."

"David? Oh yes, Hansen. We forget men have given names on the dock."

"He said it was really nice."

"It is, but a little cottage. It was the best I could do quickly. I knew I had to get you here."

"And I thank you with all my heart."

"No, I am the thankful one. I shall have a secretary. And you may not think it's all so wonderful when you see the office."

"Facing that is nothing compared to be married off to someone who was a terrible match."

He looked over at her. "Oh no! What sort of a man was he?"

"Lawrence? Oh, not a bad man, just the wrong one. But God used the whole nightmare for me to encourage him in his heart's work and to stand up to his father."

"Really? Tell me."

So she told of her work in Lawrence's life and then in Ralston's and even in Dahlia's situation."

"I think I must have the most self-sacrificing secretary anyone could wish for."

"Not at all. It was God's perfect leading and someday I will tell you what my own plan was and how silly I acted." And oh, did she act!

"You? Never."

"Oh yes, and you will laugh. I was a perfect example of how badly our own plans can be."

"Well, I will try to wait patiently for the story. But promise me if you take one look at my office and decide to go back, you'll at least tell me."

"Is the office really that bad?"

"Worse. But I will help you all I can. And you will be blessed for your hard work. That I will promise you."

Margie felt like the worst mess she could ever imagine could never be as bad as everything she'd been through. She was so grateful and was excited like a child going to the sea. She had so many things on her mind she wanted to ask Johnny.

"Johnny, you mentioned that you have no family but just before you woke up I had been searching your pockets for identification, something that I could find that would give me someone I could call. I came across a little card and wondered if it was from a family member." She held her breath waiting for a response.

"Amy? This little card?" He pulled the little card out from a pocket in his inner shirt and she nodded. "Ah, my sweet Amy."

Margie's heart plummeted. There was a beloved in his life.

"She was so precious," Johnny said. "She was my brother's adorable child. It broke my heart when the fever took her. I had so much hope built up in her as my brother and his wife had died nine days before and it seemed she was hanging on. I just didn't think God would take her, too. Now they're all in heaven together."

Margie's head lowered. "How old was she?"

"Three. A happy and sweet three. I was her Johnny. I hope someday I can have a little girl as sweet as Amy. If I dare."

Margie wondered what he meant by if he dare. There she was again with mixed emotions sorrowing for his loss and yet hopeful that perhaps a relationship could stem from their friendship.

"Oh, Johnny, it must've been awful losing them all. It must have ripped your heart out."

"Yes. I guess I clung to her as the last hope of my family. But I must trust God's judgment about who he leaves and who he takes."

"Yes, I have Jeff and Adele so far away but I don't know when I will see them."

"We're all a lonely-hearted bunch, aren't we?"

"That we are."

"I think back on that Thanksgiving together. It was certainly a miracle for all of us. I am so sorry I couldn't get you out of that house sooner."

"But Johnny, if you had, poor Dahlia would still be there and Doc would be without anyone. He seemed very happy to have Dahlia. And she was treated quite badly at my uncle's house."

"Well then, God has prevailed."

"Yes, despite my obvious lapses of faith."

"I have had a few lapses myself, especially dealing with my uncle's business. I have no comprehension why he left it to me. It wasn't as if he was angry with me." Johnny said, triggering a chuckle from Margie.

When they stopped for some snacks at a small restaurant along the way, David's conversation was mostly about Dahlia. Margie's brows raised and she looked at Johnny in agreed suspicion that the young man was very much taken with her dear friend. She was beautiful and precious. She hoped he would be worthy of her.

They settled back into the long drive and Margie began to get excited about the sea. "Tell me about Whale Rock Bay."

His eyes lit up. "It's beautiful. I am sure that you will love it if you can stand the morning fog. But even the fog has an amazing beauty. I can't wait to share it with you. There are whales spouting out to sea and dolphins, seals, otters, and well, so many things to enjoy."

"Oh!"

"The water is not blue but green blue or blue green. I can't seem to make up my mind which. But like the sea, it changes. Sometimes the sea is calm, sometimes it's wild, and in the winter it can be fierce. But I almost love that best of all. However, it wreaks havoc on the ships."

Margie was awestruck. "I can't wait to see it. Your descriptions amaze me."

"I cannot describe it. But you will soon see for yourself. It is a new way of life. I hope you will come to love it as I have."

"I am thankful for this opportunity. I think I love it already, just hearing your love of it. I am forever grateful for such a kind boss and one who loves God as I do."

He gave her the most endearing smile. One that caught her breath. How would she keep from falling in love with this man? Or had she already?

"The food is good here," Hansen said, waving them over.

And it was. But Johnny felt it was more the lovely company that made him enjoy it. It didn't take long for Hansen to bring up Dahlia again. He asked many questions of Margie, while he observed her sweet but protective responses. He enjoyed the opportunity just to look at her while she conversed with Hansen.

"Dahlia is the dearest. I have missed her friendship so much and now to be so far away."

"Perhaps she and Doc can come visit," Johnny said.

"When?" Hansen asked like an impatient child.

"I don't know. We will have to see. Doc could sleep onboard ship with us and Dahlia with Margie, I suppose," Johnny said.

Both Margie's and Hansen's countenance perked.

The travelers drove on until they were closer to the seacoast. Margie had a short nap and as she slept he noticed how lovely she was, her long lashes, warm complexion and pink lips. He'd have to keep the crew away from her. And what of his own heart?

"Can you smell it?" Johnny asked, when she woke.

"Is it the sea?"

"Yes, it's nicer up on the cliffs but a bit fishier on the docks. I hope you like to eat fish."

"I have had some I liked. I suppose I will learn."

"I am afraid you'll have to. But Rose is a great cook. She cooks meals for the whole company."

"Are there other ladies?"

"Only Rose and Lydia. And now you. I will warn you, the men are not all Christian men and even though I have filtered out some of the rougher sorts, well, I just caution you not to travel about at night."

"All right."

"Margie, do you mind my asking why the Lawrence fellow was not a suitable match?"

"First off, he didn't know our Savior. He was just a church-goer for propriety's sake. He was a banker's son with hordes of money but miserly and stingy. He was very stoic and unromantic. All business and rarely saw the world around us as I did. But he did come around after a time. His family was awful. His mother had him married to me before I even knew him."

"I see." He thought about the things she mentioned and could agree that the man was not a suitable match for her. But then would he think any man was?

Margie craned to see every new sight, like a little child. She was in awe.

"Is there snow in the winter?" she asked.

"No snow. But if you miss it, you can go inland for a drive and there it is. Myself, I think I've had enough snow for a long while."

"But we did enjoy it after we got everyone inside, didn't we?"

"I suppose we did." His smile was warm and his tone reminiscent of their short time so many months ago.

"I'll not take you to the firing squad tonight."

"The firing squad?"

"The office. It sits there like it is ready to condemn me, day after day, I'm afraid."

Margie grinned in disbelief. "You are very funny sometimes, Mr. Turner. I suppose I should call you that at work, right?"

"Johnny will be fine. It might go to my head calling me by my surname."

She rolled her eyes. Every moment with Johnny was joyous. No firing squad office would deter her. She was up for the challenge to prove her worth. Could life be any better? Only if Dahlia, Chipper and Doc were here with them. Then it would be perfect.

They drove up to the little sea cottage and it was

pure white with a sort of green-blue trim. Maybe like the sea? It was pristine and charming. And a window for her to see the ocean in all its glory.

"I hope it suits you, if not I will take you home," Johnny said, looking intently for her response.

"It's lovely. And this—this is my home, now. I plan to stay. Unless you don't want me."

She turned to look at him and he was grinning like a schoolboy. She guessed he was happy she wanted to stay.

David and Coll came in but Johnny sent Coll outside.

"She only wanted to see it," Margie said.

"Later, she'll only shed all over it. She's very good at leaving shiny black hairs everywhere. I must say, Hansen, you've done a half-nice job of it, here."

Margie was incensed. "Half-nice? Why it is a darling little cottage. I adore it."

"Thank you," David said, with a short bow.

She began to hear chattering and realized it wasn't some obscure sea creatures but Rose and Lydia coming to her with a feast.

Margie insisted the men come back and eat some of the food after they checked in because there was much too much for her.

After they left, the two ladies offered so much local information, she wasn't sure she would remember half of it. But Rose and Lydia were charming and kind.

"We figured Mr. Johnny had a sweetheart to build this little cottage for," one of them said.

"Sweetheart? Oh, no, I am but a secretary." She was embarrassed and changed the subject to their delicious meal and they left her to eat.

Margie went to the window to take in the view, but it was too dark. She would have to save her ocean tour for tomorrow. When she surveyed her little home again, she was overjoyed to see her cupboards full. How thoughtful. Perhaps when the men left after dinner, she could sit and cry tears of joy and thank God for this new life and blessing. Margie wanted to make the office a haven of thankfulness for their kindness. She couldn't wait to write Dahlia and Jeff and Adele about it.

After the two men shared the meal and left, Margie opened her trunk excited to unpack her little life into her new home. However, she only seemed to have enough energy to pull out her nightgown, slip it on, and crawl into bed. In the middle of the night she heard a strange noise but went back to sleep. Then a few hours later she heard it again but her weariness kept putting her back to sleep.

Chapter 18

The morning sky from Margie's window proved to be a light grey as fog hovered over her new world. A few streaks of morning sunlight wove their way through it. She opened the door to see more and was doused in moisture.

"So hello, Mr. Fog, you are awfully damp. I think I will enjoy you from the confines of my cottage."

She smiled at her giddiness and went back in to make some tea. The chill seemed to go right through to her bones.

She was just warming up about the time Johnny knocked.

"Good morning, it's me, Johnny," he called.

She opened the door. "Good morning."

"How do you like our fog?"

"I think he is an odd creature, but I am sure we will get along just fine."

He laughed. "Are you ready?"

"I am. I have my work clothes on."

"Then we're off."

Johnny wasn't sure what she was thinking. Her face contorted every which way. Why did the office look even worse under her scrutiny?

"It's bad. I told you. I'm sorry. The firing squad."

"It may take longer than I anticipated but it will get done. I will make it into a nice place to work."

She smiled up at him and it gave him his breath back. There was hope. Why did he doubt? She was so good and God had orchestrated this entire situation.

"Now let's start with the important papers, first—at least the ones that you know of."

He jumped to her call and came over to her. However, her close proximity was a bit unnerving. What was it about this young woman that made him want to stay right where he was and wrap her in his arms?

He abruptly went to her right side and retrieved the papers directly behind her. He pulled the papers into one big pile and shrugged his shoulders, which made her laugh.

"How have you found anything in all this?"

"The grace of God, surely."

"Are there any boxes or files I could use?"

"Yes, I remember there were several over in the corner." He sighed. "I think it is the land of no return, though." He grimaced.

"Well, if you could move the heavy boxes, then I could start sorting."

"Very well."

They worked together for some time before one sorted pile started to fall and they both went for it. Their hands touched. He didn't move. Neither did she. She looked up at him. He melted. Oh, why must she do that to me? Those beautiful eyes. He'd better do something or he'll have to kiss her. No! He can't do that. A pile fell. It broke the spell and they proceeded to pick up papers.

He swiped at the back of his neck. "I should get out of your way."

The door clanged open and two of the rougher men stood gawking at the new arrival. Well, he had warned her.

"Yes, gentlemen, what can I do for you?" Johnny asked.

"Just...they was wondering where you was and all down to the docks."

"I'll be down presently. Please close the door on the way out." One of them kept looking back in the window as they meandered back to the docks. He rolled his eyes. What if he had kissed her when they came in? He would have scandalized her on her first day. He couldn't let himself get that close.

"I think I am more of a nuisance. I will leave you to your work. But for now, I think I will lock the door. They know where to find me."

"Well, it's only one day of work." Margie surveyed her accomplishments, pleased with herself but there was a long way to go. Johnny came through the door. His cheeks were flushed with sea air and his hair wind-tossed. He was so handsome. A small gust that he brought with him sent papers flying. Margie ran to retrieve them.

"So sorry. Let me help." He gathered the few papers and when he surveyed the room, his eyes popped.

"Margie! Look what you have done. I'll never let you go now."

Johnny drew close, giving her the papers to put back in the right piles and she felt his breath on her cheek. What was this shaky feeling he gave her when he was near? She turned to look at him and he was already staring. She had no understanding of what was going on inside. She couldn't breathe. Her face was drawn to his like a magnet. He drew closer and she did not want to move away. He reached for a stray hair and the back of his fingers brushed her cheek. She felt shaky.

"Margie?" he said softly.

"Yes?"

"I've missed you all these months."

"I thought of you every time I looked out the front window toward the gate."

"Please forgive me for not coming sooner. But I'm so glad you're here. I hope you won't leave. I hope you're not just a dream."

"No, I'm very real, and extremely dusty."

"So you are. Wonderfully real. I didn't notice the dust." He smiled, offering his arm to take her back to her cottage. As they went out the door, he turned to her. "Even dusty you're beautiful."

Oh, she wasn't expecting that. He looked boyish and shy. Had he never said these kind of words to a woman before?

"I am very impressed with what you have accomplished in one day."

"We'll have the office looking regal in no time."

"We? Hardly we. You have done this. You, dear lass, have a true gift for this."

As they walked toward the cottage, she shivered. "I am not used to this damp sort of cold. I think I may need to knit a heavier sweater."

Johnny took off his coat and wrapped it around her

shoulders. "Whatever you need, you shall have it. Men travel back and forth every day to the cities down the south coast. There are many things they can get you. They would be inept at choosing your manner of supplies but if you write a note they can take it to the store's proprietor and they will get what you need. Businesses often send the ladies samples to gain more patronage."

"I see. Then I shall talk to Lydia and Rose."

"Good. And don't hold back for you shall have a bonus after this job."

"But, Johnny, what about the cottage? I have a lot of work to pay you back."

"Never. It is part of your job. A secretary has to have somewhere to board."

She cocked her head. "I am a spoiled secretary."

Johnny lingered for a few seconds then opened her door. She thanked him and gave him his coat. She shut the door, drew the drapes and sat until she remembered how dirty she was. What a day! She would sleep tonight. And she did until that strange noise sounded again.

It was so clear that Johnny could see the far side of the bay as if it were near as he walked up the hill to the office. The white caps dotted the sea, ever moving as if trying to escape each other. He opened the door to what could no longer be termed the firing squad, for the lovely little secretary had tamed its condemning ways into conformity and peace. What would she manage today? He shook his head. She was a wonder.

Margie came in smiling. She seemed motivated to get to her job. He sighed. He was going to have to face her. They said their good mornings and plans and he stopped her before she started to work.

"Margie, I owe you an apology for my behavior last night."

"Whatever for?" She looked at him incredulously. She didn't know?

"I felt as if I was being ungentlemanly. I apologize."

"I did not take anything as ungentlemanly last night."

Bright innocent eyes did nothing but unnerve him and he was speechless. Perhaps all of his feelings were not showing as he thought. He nodded and left her to her work to go down to the docks.

Father, what is this? I never felt like this. When she's there I feel so drawn to her, and when she's gone, she's all I think about. I am not sure I should be around her at all and yet I want to be.

Why did he feel as if God was smiling at him?

As he walked across the docks, some of the men

were grinning at him as if they knew what sort of things he was battling inside.

"New secretary sure is pretty," one of them said.

"Yep. Sure is. Wish you'd bring some more like her this way, boss," said another.

Johnny climbed aboard ship in search of Hansen.

"Morning, Boss," Hansen said. "You all right? You look a little out of sorts."

"Hansen?"

"Yes, Boss?"

"You seem to like Dahlia."

"Oh yes, sir."

"Tell me, why do I feel like this?" He grabbed a magnet and put it atop the ship's compass.

Hansen looked perplexed.

"What happens when I do this?"

"It takes over the compass and it won't read correctly. The guys call it haywire."

"Well, this is what this lovely secretary does to me when I am in the same vicinity with her. I am all over the place. My thoughts are jumbled, my arms want to reach for her. I say one thing and mean another. Yes, haywire."

Johnny could see that Hansen was trying not to smile. He should never have said a thing to him.

"Sir, have you never been in love?"

"Love? Is that what it is? But it's so— unruly."

Hansen finally laughed. "Don't worry, sir, I'm not

laughing at you but with you. I am in the same predicament with Miss Dahlia. However, I have been in love before as a young lad. All the signs are there."

"Signs?"

"Yes. Well now, let's see. There is that compass thing," he said, pointing to the compass. "And you miss her so much you can't stand it. All your thoughts and everything you do are saying, she will love this or she will enjoy that. It gets to be meddling."

Johnny nodded. "Oh, yes, meddling."

"And you feel like you would practically die to get to the time where you see her again. And everything you do starts being for her benefit. You job, your money, your own upkeep. Yes, sir there are a lot of signs." He whistled.

"But I cannot."

"Cannot what?"

"Love her."

"Why ever not?"

"Because I don't want to lose her."

"Is that supposed to make sense?"

"Yes. No. Everyone in my family died. I couldn't bear to give my heart again."

"And you cannot bear not to, sir. Even if God takes someone, you still have the joy of that time with them."

"To haunt me the rest of my life?"

"No, sir, no. To know that you had something

beautiful and special and to think back on the blessing."

"But it is too painful. I don't want to hurt like that. I can't let this happen. Perhaps I should send her back."

"You can't. You promised, sir. And where would you send her?"

"That's true. I cannot send her back. Then I must stay away from her."

"Good luck, sir."

"That is the way it needs to be."

Why did Hansen have that knowing smirk on his face? He thinks I can't do this, that I can't forget her, let her go. I can. I think.

Chapter 19

Johnny came to a halt when he stepped through the door. What has she done?

"Gentlemen, I'm finally getting to the cleaning in here. I hope it looks a bit better," Margie said.

Hansen whistled.

"I am speechless," Johnny said, this time for a different reason.

"Did you call in the cavalry while we were gone?" Hansen asked looking around.

Margie giggled.

The place was amazing. How did she ever accomplish it?

"Wow! I didn't expect this. We wanted to come up and invite you to eat at Rose's," Johnny said. "She sent a message to everyone that she had made a huge pot of stew and biscuits."

"Yes, she mentioned it to me, too, but I hated to quit."

The two men stepped toward her and escorted her toward the door.

"Let's go, Margie." Johnny gave his arm and Hansen opened the door. Margie untied her apron and tossed it.

"I guess I'm going to lunch then." She looked up at him, her eyes smiling more than her mouth.

"Seems to be the case," Johnny said, sighing.

Here he was again arm in arm with her and he was supposed to be ignoring her. But how could he? Her closeness flustered him. He could smell some sort of intoxicating concoction of sea air, musty papers and maybe light perfume.

"I really should stop and wash up."

"You can do that at Rose's. She has a washstand and plenty of towels. Makes everyone wash up," Hansen said.

"But I don't need much to eat…" Margie looked from Hansen to Johnny, trying to convince them.

"Nonsense. You'll be blowing out to sea, with all your hard work and no food," Johnny said.

She laughed. "Well, perhaps I am a bit hungry."

"I'm taking no chances with my amazing secretary."

Margie went straight over to Rose and Lydia and

began to help them serve. Many of the men took their bowls and sat out on the porch, but Margie and the women along with Johnny and David and two other men, sat at a table together.

"Have you met Chowder and Friedman?" Rose asked her.

"No. How do you do?"

"Just fine," Chowder said.

"Glad to meet you Miss Margie. Heard a lot about ya," Friedman said, blushing like a schoolgirl.

"What had you heard?" she asked him.

"Only that you were a topnotch secretary." The man grinned at her and winked at Johnny

"We're certainly happy you are here," Lydia said, scooping some stew into her mouth. "Ouch, that's a bit hot."

"How do you do it Rose? The meat melts in my mouth. You are a great cook. My friend Dahlia would so enjoy cooking with you."

At the mention of Dahlia, David dropped his spoon into his bowl. "Yes, she's a grand cook too," he said, fishing his spoon out of his stew.

He looked up at Johnny and Johnny pointed at him. "See?"

She wondered what they were talking about. When Johnny saw her looking at him, he frowned. Why did he do that? Was he unhappy with her? Perhaps he was afraid she was like Rose and Lydia trying to nab a husband. Well, she'd make sure he knew that was not the reason she came. So as soon as she finished, she tried to help Rose and Lydia and they refused her so she excused herself and scooted right back out the door to the office.

She grabbed her apron and set back to work, but her heart was heavy. Had he not felt what she felt when they were so close the other night? Did he think she was unrighteous in her behavior? Was her desire to let him kiss her obvious? She hoped not.

The anxiousness of her heart paid off in her working extremely hard until closing. She had all the walls clean and most of the floor. The walls that had been pale green proved to be white and the whole office started to shine.

Johnny was not there to walk her home so she went on alone. When sadness tried to creep in, she focused on her progress for the day instead.

Rose had stopped by and set out a piece of fried cod that Margie was sure was far too large until she started eating and never stopped. How had she gained such an appetite?

She rested and finally wrote a very long letter to Jeff and Adele. She hoped they weren't too anxious about her.

When she crawled into bed, she lay there hearing

the crashing waves. It was such a strange sound yet soothing. She wondered if Johnny would show her around as he promised. He seemed so distant today. Perhaps he felt she was being unladylike, nearly being intoxicated with his face so close the other day. She decided not to think about it and her thoughts went to Dahlia and Doc and how they were getting along. She smiled to think how David seemed rather taken with her dear friend. Then she began to think about Chipper. Poor Chipper. She longed to envelope the dear lone boy in her arms and give him a home. If only she could.

Tomorrow she would write Dahlia and tell her how she had been transforming the firing squad. She knew Dahlia would be very anxious to hear from her.

She wondered about her uncle's family and Lawrence. They were most likely angry but she had done all she could. She left the beautiful gowns and thanked them for the nice things that they did. She also sent a message to Lawrence and thanked him for his consideration but gently ended their relationship except to pray for him.

Then the foghorn sounded. Johnny had laughed when she asked what it was. It was an eerie sort of sound and yet comforting. But she was still alone even in the charming little sea cottage. She wondered what kind of things she could create to make it her own. Would she be here long? She hoped so for there was no going back. Best not to think on that, but be thankful, and she was.

She had prayed this morning for everyone but tonight she was determined to be purely thankful.

Thank you, Father, for who you are, for being an amazing God and King. My heart's desire is to serve and love you all my days. And to obey your Word and serve you by serving your children.

On Sundays, those who desired would meet either outside if sunny or inside at Rose's to share the Word. There was no church or parson, so Johnny usually shared and the younger Christians sometimes asked questions. Happily today was sunny and they met out on a soft bluff with old quilts for the ladies to sit on.

Johnny greeted everyone and they sang some hymns. She watched as he opened his Bible. He seemed excited to share.

"Friends, the Lord gave me this during my prayer time this week and I was so blessed that I wanted to share it. Here we sit with the sea before us and all of us have talked about the sea being a testimony of God's power. So read with me in Psalm 107 verses twenty-one through thirty-one:

'Oh that men would praise the LORD for his goodness, and
for his wonderful works to the children of men!
And let them sacrifice the sacrifices of thanksgiving, and
declare his works with rejoicing.
They that go down to the sea in ships, that do business in
great waters;
These see the works of the LORD, and his wonders in the
deep.
For he commandeth, and raiseth the stormy wind, which
lifteth up the waves thereof.
They mount up to the heaven, they go down again to the
depths: their soul is melted because of trouble.
They reel to and fro, and stagger like a drunken man, and are
at their wit's end.
Then they cry unto the LORD in their trouble, and he
bringeth them out of their distresses.
He maketh the storm a calm, so that the waves thereof are
still.
Then are they glad because they be quiet; so he bringeth
them unto their desired haven.
Oh that men would praise the LORD for his goodness, and
for his wonderful works to the children of men!'

This is us, dear friends. We are those that go down to
the sea in ships and do business in the great waters. We
have seen his hand even at shore when he lifts the waves
and they reel and stagger like a drunken man. Our lives
can be driven like the sea waves. We cry out to Him in
our distress and he comes to us and makes our lives a

calm. And some he brought here as a desired haven."

Margie was in awe. That was her story. Her life was in such a turmoil and all looked so bleak and hopeless. But God brought her here and gave her peace in this desired haven. Tears were starting to come and it was a good thing that others had asked for prayer. She was able to discretely wipe them away.

Everyone seemed touched by Johnny. His voice seemed to take on a certain authority and yet so humble and kind. She loved these times. He was much like her father and much like her Lord. He looked at her, knowingly, gently. He knew the words were for her heart. She turned and looked out to sea. It was calm and streaks of sunlight lit the edges of the waves and they looked like glass. When she looked up, most everyone had left and Johnny came to sit next to her.

"It was so beautiful," she said.

"The sea?"

"No, what you shared. It touched my heart."

"I thought it might. This has been a haven for both of us."

"Thank you for sharing it."

"What I shared was from the Lord, not me, today."

"I know. I could see it. I could feel it. The sea is a picture of our lives."

"His creation is a testimony of who he is and as I look

out to sea, I see myself so small and insignificant."

"Yet he knows the number of hairs on our head." She smiled up at him. He reached to brush the hair away from her face. And she wanted his hand to stay right there on her face and let her feel the warmth and comfort of it.

It was the end of the week. The men were given two days off between shipments so Johnny decided to keep his promise to Margie.

"Bring a warm wrap with you. I'm not sure how the weather will be."

He had Rose make a picnic lunch and they were off. They traveled by car up the coast and walked along pathways to the cliffs.

"I asked Hansen, or David, along but he insisted he had something else to do."

"I imagine if Dahlia were here, it would be another story," Margie said, making them both chuckle.

"Yes, I think you're right on that account."

"I wrote her a couple of days ago. I'll be glad to hear from her."

"You must be lonely, working alone in the office all day and at home in your cottage at night."

"A little I suppose. But I'm very happy, really. I love

the sea and the fog and the laughing gulls."

"Yes, those silly seagulls. They are always around when I drop something or stumble and it is as if they saw me and start laughing."

"How funny," Margie said.

They made it down closer to the edge of the cliff and laid their picnic down.

"What a view. Look at the waves crashing against that rock!" She was enamored just as he was when he first came to the sea. It did his heart good.

"Yes, isn't it wonderful. I have come to love this place."

"It's glorious. I see God's handiwork in every direction. I want to know about every tree and flower and creature."

Johnny laughed. "You'll learn. I have not even begun to put a name to everything."

"Johnny?" Margie turned to him.

"Yes?"

"May I ask you something and will you be honest with me in your answer?"

"Of course."

"The other evening when you and I…were alone at the office," she looked down rubbing her fingers together. "Did you feel I also was being um… inappropriate?"

"You? Of course not. I would never think that of you.

175

It was all me. I was inappropriate." He looked out to sea. How could she think she did anything wrong?

"But you were not, Johnny. Yet you barely spoke to me afterward."

"I'm sorry. I surely didn't mean to be aloof. I was honestly trying not to put you in a position like that again."

"What do you mean?"

"I'm not sure it was proper to have been so close."

She gulped. "Oh, you think it would have been wrong?"

"I don't know. I only know, my dear friend, that I did not want you to leave because of my bad behavior."

"I'll not leave."

"But I am not sure of my passion when I am near you. That I might not try—to—kiss you." There he said it.

"Oh." Margie turned away from him and faced the sea.

"I've embarrassed us both."

"No. It's fine. I've never felt this way. It is as much my fault as it is yours."

Just that minute a couple of gulls flew over laughing.

"They found us." It broke the intensity of the discussion and they laughed back at them and had their lunch.

"Did Rose think we'd be gone for a week?"

"She surely packed a lot in this basket." Margie pulled out wonderful treasures, even a blackberry pie.

"They grow all over in the outlying areas."

"What does?"

"Blackberries."

"I see. How nice. Did she think we would eat the whole pie?"

"We'll want to but it's ill-advised," Johnny said, smiling.

"Rose is a wonderful cook."

"Yes, we'll build her a restaurant as soon as we start bringing in more money."

"Are any of the men married?"

"Only one. His wife is in the next harbor waiting for him to build them a house."

"I hope she will be able to come soon."

"He has started on the house. I will drive you by the housing area on the way back."

She nodded happily as she chewed her sandwich.

"Are you happy here, Margie?"

"Very. I love your sea, Johnny."

His heart leapt. He never wanted her to leave.

After their lunch, they climbed down the bluff.

"How you doing?"

"I think my shoes are not good for this," she said, slipping.

"No, perhaps we need to go down another day. Look!"

"What?"

"Here, stand by me and follow my arm and watch that area. He'll come back up soon. Look for a spray of white sea water."

"I see it. What is it?"

"A whale."

"A whale. As in Jonah?"

"Yes." He laughed at her charming child-like excitement.

"Oh, Johnny, it is all so wonderful." She looked up at him with those tender eyes and he was transfixed. He put his hands at her waist and felt her breath catch. The wind kicked up and he turned her toward the sea—her back against him, her hair blowing in his face. They watched together for new whale sightings.

Holding her felt so good, so right, somehow. Solomon's words in the book of Proverbs came to him as he fought hard not to turn her around and kiss her. "There be three things which are too wonderful for me, yea, four which I know not: The way of an eagle in the air; the way of a serpent upon a rock; the way of a ship in the midst of the sea; and the way of a man with a maid." He was finally beginning to understand the last part and it was too much for him to comprehend as well.

Margie shivered in his arms.

"Are you cold?"

"Yes. I'm still not used to this dampness. It seems colder than the snow we were in."

He wrapped his arms around her and turned her into his chest.

"Is that warmer?" he asked, breathing in the scent of her hair, her hat in her hand.

"Yes," she said and stopped shivering. She looked up into his face, her cheeks rosy from the sea breeze.

He couldn't fight it any longer. "May I kiss you?"

She looked up at him in sweet innocence. "I have never been kissed, though a couple have tried."

"I would be the first to ever kiss you?" He pondered the power of that first kiss. It would be his as well.

She assented by a nod. She was irresistible.

"I don't know then, if I am worthy of the honor." He spoke the words in a daze. He wanted to kiss her. He was completely haywire.

"Oh, Johnny."

He pulled her closer and his lips barely brushed hers like a feather and he pulled away. He couldn't. He nestled her back into his embrace and held her there. They stood silently for a long time. Until he could commit to her, he would not kiss her. He set his chin on her head and savored the moment.

The breeze turned into a wind and they climbed back to the top and took one last look at the vast sea.

"It's a testimony of God's creation," Margie said.

"It is. His power and majesty." He turned to her. "I am so glad you like my sea, Margie. It's yours too now."

"I do. It's fascinating."

"Not as much as you are."

She looked at him with honor in her eyes. Was it honor at him not kissing her? Was it for the compliment? Did she understand he honored her?

As they drove home, he was beginning to compare the sea's power to love's power. Love certainly was a strong and powerful entity. After all, it was love that gave mankind new life through the sacrifice of the Son of God.

FOR GOD SO LOVED THE WORLD, THAT HE GAVE HIS ONLY BEGOTTEN SON, THAT WHOSOEVER BELIEVETH IN HIM SHOULD NOT PERISH, BUT HAVE EVERLASTING LIFE.

Yes, Lord. Pure love in John 3:16.

Well, Solomon, there is another to ponder about.

Johnny stood staring at the ship's compass, running his fingers through his hair.

I couldn't resist her, Lord. She's like a magnet and I feel like that compass spinning out of control. I didn't kiss her but oh, how I wanted to. I just don't want to hurt. I don't think I can stand to lose one more person.

LOVE IS A SACRIFICE.

He pondered on the word the Lord said all day long, working through all of his fears. And then the Lord spoke again.

DID YOU NOT ASK TO BE RELIEVED OF YOUR LONELINESS?

He hung his head. Of course he had, so many times. The Lord had broken through but now he had new concerns. Why would she want to marry him? He had nothing to offer her. But he knew, somehow he knew, she was his perfect match. He remembered the funny look on her face when he woke up from his dormant sleep. He thought he was in heaven and there was this beautiful creature waiting for him to wake.

He must look at his funds. He must ask her before someone else did. Another thing to worry about. Would she marry anyone else? He didn't think so; she seemed so content in his arms but perhaps she was just cold. But oh, how the plague of loneliness disappeared when she was near.

Chapter 20

Margie and Johnny were both late for work the next morning. As Johnny opened the door, he asked Hansen if he'd bring them some tea.

"Thank you." Margie said. "I barely had time to dress this morning. I even missed my devotions. I didn't sleep much."

So she didn't sleep well because of yesterday either. "I'm sorry," Johnny said. "You should have rested and come in later. Take some time out of the day. I didn't sleep well myself."

"Johnny, I have a question for you. I know we don't have much to offer but do you think someday we might be able to bring Dahlia and Doc here to live?"

"I've thought of it many times since we left, but they need a place to live. The bluff I showed you is protected from the heavy winds and I've had my eye on it for some time. The pines make a perfect windbreak for some homes. But I have little to work with. Nearly everything I have has been invested into this business."

"I thought as much. We will have to trust God." She appeared sad but not disheartened.

"My heart is that we should all be together for Thanksgiving."

"Chipper too?"

"Of course. He is always in my prayers."

"He adores you, Johnny."

"He thinks you're a peach. I believe that's what he said."

He reached for her hand and kissed it.

"God will make a way," she said, blushing.

She looked up at him with her sparkling brown eyes and long lashes and it made him sigh in delight that she might be his.

At lunch he brought soup and bread as she finished the last of the real scrubbing.

"You have done miraculous things with the firing squad. I am not intimidated in the least anymore."

They laughed and she thanked him humbly, sweetly, as she always did.

The room looked like a big city office. The furniture, he once felt needed to be burned looked new. It was shiny, the wood grain restored.

"The only thing we need now is one more small desk."

"I shall be on it right away. In the meantime our

soup is getting cold."

They sat devouring the cream of broccoli soup and homemade rolls.

"What would we do without Rose?" Margie said.

"I have no idea. God gave her as a great gift to all of us."

"Yes, Dahlia is gifted that way too. They could work together. She and Rose would get along perfectly. Neither are bossy."

"Sounds as if we're going to have a whole community here. Even a doctor."

"Yes, but we mustn't overwork him."

"These old salts are tough and the women, too. He'd have little to do, I think."

They joyfully plotted and planned their new town for weeks when Johnny wasn't called down the coast on business.

Dahlia had been conversing with David by letters and that made Margie deliciously mischievous for matching them up again.

She prayed daily for all of them, the ones far and near. Even for Lawrence and Ralston and the rest of her uncle's family. She wouldn't forget the one who was constantly on her mind. She had missed him terribly. The trips had been agonizing. If it hadn't been for Coll, she'd have been miserable. She thought about the happy town they planned and tried to keep her mind set in that direction and do all that she could to help his business run smoothly. She thought about what they would name this new town. One thing she knew for certain—it needed to give God glory.

It was Johnny's fourth trip out of town and it lasted longer than she thought she could stand. Sometimes he went by ship and sometimes he drove down the coast. Each way was equally dangerous, but sometimes he needed to meet with those who were on the receiving end and were processing the fish catches. She closed the office door and started to walk home, when she saw some of the people pointing toward the road.

"It's the boss," someone yelled and her heart did somersaults. She hurried to the back and saw Johnny as he opened the back door for someone. Dahlia!

She ran to her squealing as Johnny stood laughing.

"She's happier to see you than me, I think," he said, pretending to pout.

"She is one I can properly hug, Johnny," Margie said.

"Not forever," he mumbled happily, retrieving Dahlia's suitcase.

Margie kept those words in her heart and reached for her friend.

"Dahlia, can you stay long? What about Doc? Is he okay?"

"I'm just fine," Doc called out from the other side of the car.

"What? Doc!" Margie squealed, running around to the other side giving him a big hug.

"Another one she can properly hug," Johnny mumbled.

She looked up at Johnny. He shrugged and smiled.

She would have loved to have run into his arms, but she didn't dare. Not yet.

"He goes off and leaves me over and over and I'm supposed to be happy every time he comes back," Margie teased back at him.

"Aren't you pleased this time?"

"So very pleased, thank you."

The five of them sat for a meal of crispy halibut and potato latkes and spinach salad with walnuts from the inland valley.

Dahlia kept looking over to David and David to Dahlia and Margie to Johnny and back. Doc started to laugh and they all realized why.

"Have you seen Chipper?" Margie asked.

"Yes, and he is well but coming of an age that will throw him out into the factories," Doc said.

Margie's heart sank but she would not give up hope for the boy.

After their meal, Johnny walked over to the window. Margie followed, stood on her tiptoes and whispered in Johnny's ear. "Is it permanent?" she asked.

"No, just a visit. I thought we could manage."

"I'm so glad." And when she saw no one was looking, she gave him a little peck on his cheek.

He grinned. "You're blushing," he whispered.

She grinned back. "Yes, you are."

"Here's dessert, folks. Boss's favorite," Rose carried in a lemon meringue pie and Lydia brought the plates.

After the scrumptious pie, everyone retired, but Margie and Dahlia chatted late into the night about the wonders of their hearts.

"Do you think Johnny will ask you to marry?" Dahlia asked.

"I think so. He has certainly acted the part of the suitor."

"I'm so happy. To think of you married to Lawrence Parkerson makes me turn inside out," Dahlia said.

Her comment struck Margie as hilarious and she couldn't stop laughing. Then Dahlia started in, but it was broken up by the loud blare of the foghorn.

"What's that?" Dahlia said.

"Just the foghorn. You'll hear it all night until you get used to it. Kind of like the chimes of a grandfather's clock. And by the way, tell me about your correspondence with David?"

"I look forward to them so much. He's told me of his life and I have been telling him of mine. He's a good man." She sparkled as she talked about him.

"Johnny thinks I questioned him unmercifully about David the moment I knew he had eyes for you."

Dahlia was all shades of pink on her ivory skin, her blue eyes wide with surprise.

"Does everybody know?"

"No, but after today, I would venture to say they have a clue from the blue-eyed couple mooning over each other."

Dahlia's mouth dropped and Margie giggled.

"We're like two schoolgirls, you and me."

They climbed into bed and Margie lay there smiling. Would there be future wedding bells for them both? And could the whole beloved group be together for always?

But what about Chipper, Father? We must have him, too. Save him from the workhouses. Please, Lord!

"Isn't it amazing?" Margie swept her arm across the expanse of the sea.

"It is," Dahlia said. "I was going to say it's beautiful and big and frightening. Is there a word for this?"

"I don't know but it certainly is all that. I have come

to love it."

"I would love to be here with everyone, but I couldn't leave Doc. He'd be so lonely. He's been happy with my company. He is like the father I always wished I had."

"Then we must get him here, too. Johnny wants to bring the whole lot of us up here but he is so frustrated without funds to build houses for everyone. He needs more workers, too. But they need homes and decent places for their families to live in."

"We need a miracle."

"We do, friend." Margie put her arm through Dahlia's and showed her a whale spout.

"A whale. Imagine. And with the men out there. Won't the whale swallow them up?"

"No," Margie said, starting to laugh. "The whales actually prefer fish."

"I'll not go out there."

"You'll not have to. The men must go out and sometimes in very rough seas so we must pray for them."

"I certainly will." Dahlia's face was stone grey and serious, staring out to sea.

"I'll miss you when you go. I hope we can do this again soon. Johnny is so busy, we cannot take the time to go visit you."

"He could send you, perhaps."

"By way of a certain blue-eyed admirer I suppose?" Margie teased, bringing the color back into Dahlia's cheeks.

"That would be pleasant, of course."

"You are as silly as I am."

"You? Tell me does your heart pound fiercely when you get close to Johnny?"

"Like it's going to jump off a cliff," Margie said.

"It is strange feeling like this. I only felt something similar when a stableman came to a place I was working. But he only had eyes for his horses."

"He was a fool! I am sure David Hansen would agree."

"It's getting cold."

"See the fog?"

"Where?'

"The big blanket roll sitting out over the sea. It is coming in and if we don't get back soon we'll be damp."

They barely made it back before it came in.

"It came so fast."

"Yes, I had to learn that the hard way, hanging clothes out."

"It is a new world here," Dahlia said, as she, Margie and Rose sat in the cottage, watching the fog. "And your cottage is so nice. David is a good carpenter."

"Yes, he is."

"How was it paid for?"

"I never thought to ask. I suppose the business. But then it wasn't making much money then."

Rose looked up. "I can tell you. It came out of Mr. Johnny's own funds."

"Oh my," Margie said, putting her hand to her heart.

"But I think he must be happy with the investment as I've seen that office you have reconstructed," Rose said.

"Was it that bad?" Dahlia asked.

Rose and Margie looked at each other and rolled their eyes.

"You can't imagine, Dahlia."

"It was a site none of us wanted to touch. I was glad I was a cook," Rose said, smiling.

"I'll miss you. It's been so good. So perfect having you here."

Johnny knew Margie was holding back her tears. How he wished he could get them up here to live quickly, but only a miracle could do it. He assigned Hansen to take them back at Margie's urging. Of course Hansen and Dahlia seemed quite happy with that arrangement. Doc had a wonderful time talking with the old salts, fishing a little with Hansen and talking about godly things with Johnny as they slept aboard ship. But it gave Johnny a feel of how Doc would like being here at the sea.

They waved them off and then turned to each other.

"It's all right, you know."

"What is?" she said.

"Crying a few tears."

"Oh." She looked down. He raised her chin, took out his handkerchief, and wiped her cheeks gently.

"I want them here as badly as you do, Margie. I'll do everything I can."

"I know, Johnny. You are a dear. I can't thank you enough for this visit."

"It was good to see them. But I suppose I'd better get this shipping business shipshape so we can do something about it."

"Yes, sir, Boss." Margie saluted, making them both laugh.

Chapter 21

By the time the office was pleasant enough for Margie's liking, a big horse-drawn wagon came pounding down the road toward the building. She watched as Johnny ran out to meet them. He directed them as they carried something toward the office.

"Right over here," Johnny said.

The burly men set down a beautiful piece of furniture.

He thanked them and turned to her. "Well, Margie, what do you think?"

"It's beautiful."

"It's your new desk."

"Mine?"

"You said you needed a desk."

"Yes, but a small one, nothing this elaborate."

"You deserve it. You are the most amazing secretary anyone could have. I'd build you your own office except that I wouldn't be able to look at you every day."

She walked over to the desk, trying to avoid his grin, her heart full at such a comment. Every time she looked up it was still there. It seemed to be stuck on his face. He was like a big boy watching over her every move. And she was like a little girl imagining all the wonderful things she could put in the drawers. It was hand-carved perfection. She ran her hand across the top of the smooth top and looked over at him. He was still grinning.

"Johnny, you built me a house. You didn't need to do this."

"I sure did. Do you like it? Will it do?"

She wanted to run into his arms and thank him. But she just looked into his eyes and thanked him with all her heart.

"Have a good time putting your desk together, my lovely secretary," he said, walking out the door, still grinning.

"Oh, Johnny, you're the best," she said looking toward the dock.

"The mail's here," Johnny said, plopping the sack on his desk.

"I'll sort it," Margie said hoping for a letter from Dahlia.

"Okay, I'll send one of the boys up to get their mail in about an hour."

He shut the door and she scurried to go through the mail. She didn't want to be silly about it, but she was itching to hear. It had been a while since Dahlia or Jeff had written.

There was only a letter from Doc to Johnny. She waited impatiently until he came back.

When he came back, he brought back lunch from Rose's.

"There is a letter from Doc to you."

He grabbed it with the other men's mail and left.

He was going to cause her to have a conniption fit.

"Well?" she said after he came back.

"Well, what?"

"Doc's letter?"

"Oh, I forgot," he said, pulling it out of his pocket.

She sighed and waited, tapping her fingers on her new desk.

His countenance fell.

"What is it? Is it Dahlia?"

"No, it's Chipper. They are starting to train him for the factory."

"Oh, no! Johnny, we have to do something."

She rose from her chair and Johnny from his. He reached for her hand. She thought he was going to pray but he just told her to get her coat and hat and he'd be right back.

"Do I need something to write on?"

"No, come on."

His demeanor was no-nonsense. She just obeyed.

They rode along in the car to the north cliffs and stopped. He led her down to the place where they had picnicked. She loved it here. The sun was peaking through the clouds and the waves crashed softly below.

He turned her to face him, his face almost stern and intense. A far cry from the grinning schoolboy earlier.

"Margie, you must know by now, I have fallen in love with you and I love every little thing about you. My life is fully yours. There is nothing I want more than to court you in proper ways and build you a big beautiful home but…"

He pushed the hair out of his face and continued. "But there is this problem."

She was afraid. Was there someone else?

"Problem?" she said, barely audible.

"No, no, not a problem, exactly."

He started to pace, then stopped to face her again. "Margie?"

"Yes?"

"It's the boy, Chipper. He needs someone to adopt him and if we were married, then…"

"Oh, honestly, Johnny. Is that what this is all about?"

"Yes, I've said it."

"You do want to marry me, don't you?"

"Oh, blundering fool that I am. Of course I do. Chipper or not."

"Then I would be glad to marry you and adopt Chipper."

His face lit up. "Really? You would?"

"Of course. I would marry you to save Chipper but I love you already."

"I should have known."

He wrapped her in his arms and held her tightly. She snuggled her head up to his ear. "Yes, you should have."

He pushed her just far enough away to look into her eyes.

"Of course, of course, my beautiful Marguerite," he said. Then he drew her face close and kissed her forehead and cheek until he came to her lips. It was like the power of the waves crashing to shore.

The foghorn sounded as they came out of their own fog and a huge ray of sunlight spread its glory onto the place where they stood.

He picked her up in his arms and kissed her again. She wrapped her arms around him, overwhelmed with joy.

He carried her to the car, stopping every so often to kiss her again, then he set her inside and they journeyed on beginning to make plans for their new life.

Chapter 22

"He's a mess."

"Naw, he's a fool."

"Well, I think it's dandy. Have me a wife someday."

"Not me. Too much trouble."

Johnny laughed at the boys on the dock, as they assessed his happy countenance. Oh, but won't I be happy to have beautiful, sweet Margie as my wife. No, he was no fool!

"You don't think they are saying we are only getting married for Chipper's sake, do you?" Margie asked him, earlier.

Johnny was nearly hysterical with laughing as he tried to answer. "Don't you know they had us both pegged from the day I brought you here?"

He remembered that day. It was as if he had brought his betrothed home to his new land. He just hadn't been sure she'd stay. He was so afraid to lose her, and what a horrible mess he'd saddled her with. She'd not said one bad thing about it. He would have to make up for that the rest of his life.

He continued up the hill and met Rose who was bringing some tarts down to the men.

"Sure wish you could have married here, Mr. Johnny. Would have been a lovely wedding but I am glad you'll let us have a nice party when you come home."

"We'd love to be here, Rose, but there are papers to sign and no parson."

"I know, but God bless it all and I look forward to seeing the boy. I'll be fattening the lad up for certain."

"He is going to love you, Rose." Johnny smiled all the way up the hill at the thought of Chipper being fattened up and happy.

Then he saw Margie, standing in her traveling jacket. A lovely thing she made in colors of the sea, she told him.

Coll came to meet him. "Sorry girl, not this trip, but when you see who I am bringing back, you will be one happy dog." He ruffed up her hair and squatted to shake her paw. She was so smart. How perfectly God had used her to help bring this family of lonely-hearted people together. "Rose will spoil you, so no pouting, you hear?" Coll barked, wagging her tail and nuzzling at his hand.

The trip went quickly for them as they shared their lives and dreams freely. They spoke of their early encounters and meetings and the way they really felt.

"I was enamored right from the beginning," Margie said, still a little unsure of sharing her emotions.

"With me?"

"Oh, yes, you were in my thoughts all the time. Poor Lawrence didn't have a chance. No one could match up to you."

Johnny whistled. "Boy, if I knew that I would have asked sooner."

"What about that night in the office?"

He shook his head. "I felt so out of line. I wanted to kiss you so badly. I was acting like a compass."

"A what?"

"I told myself you were a magnet and I was a compass. I took the magnet to Hansen and said what happens when this magnet comes in contact with the compass. Well, one day I will show you but the compass is all over the place. He said the boys call it haywire. When I got near you I was out of control. Needed to go back and find my bearings."

She blushed at his stories and yet they made her feel so loved and wanted.

"I wanted you to kiss me," she said shyly.

"I thought as much. That is why I couldn't go on.

And I didn't want any problems with your impeccable reputation."

"And I thought you were angry with me."

"Never, you poor darling. I could never be angry with you."

"You look heavenly. What a beautiful dress," Dahlia said.

"It was my mother's," Margie said. "I made it fit for a more simple ceremony." It had been like cutting off her hair to trim the dress but it could be put back together for a daughter someday, if she so desired.

Dahlia finished up the last touches of Margie's tendrils that hung from the charming hat Johnny bought her.

"Stunning."

"If I am, it is because of you. dear friend."

The hat was a warm white with soft pink cabbage roses all around woven in by white and pink tulle. Dahlia had pulled a bit of tulle and baby's breath and with a few roses made a lovely bouquet.

"I'll go tell Doc you are ready."

She was so glad for Dahlia to be her maid of honor and Doc to walk her down the short aisle.

There were few people there to see it. She had invited her family but was not expecting them, but as she came down the aisle, she saw Ralston. She smiled at him. Then she turned her head to walk to her groom and there he was grinning like that silly schoolboy again. She wanted to laugh. But when he got a better look at her, his mouth dropped and he looked stunned. She walked into his arm. He was so tall and stately in his suit, her heart flipped. Her husband, her Johnny.

The parson spoke of the relationship of Christ and his bride and a man and his wife and it touched her heart.

When the moment to kiss the bride came, Johnny gently kissed her and whispered his love in her ear.

Ralston congratulated Johnny and kissed her on the cheek. "You look radiant, Cuz."

"I am so happy, Ralston."

"So am I. I am leaving home. I've found a place to hire me as an apprentice. I'll be in the south full swing in the shipbuilding business."

"Really?" Johnny said. "We need to stay in contact."

"Johnny has a shipping business, Ralston," Margie said.

"Oh, I will," Ralston said, shaking Johnny's hand vigorously. "You have an amazing bride, sir. She changed my direction and I am forever indebted."

"I only did what God showed me to do," Margie

said.

"I know I am very blessed. I too, am indebted— for life." Johnny grinned at her.

"Will you come and visit us, Ralston?" Margie said.

"I would love to."

"Perhaps for Thanksgiving," Johnny said with a laugh.

"When do we get to go home?" Chipper said looking up at them, his bright eyes full of joy.

"In a few days. We are waiting for all the legalities," Johnny said. "But at least you can stay with Doc for part of the time."

"All right." Chipper was so anxious. It broke her heart to tell him to wait.

"Come on, Chipper. Let's go finish the wedding feast," Dahlia said.

The boy roused and followed Dahlia and Doc, and the newlyweds had a few moments together before they went to Doc's house for dinner.

"It was a lovely wedding," Margie said.

"Not the kind you may have liked to have."

"That is silly, Johnny. All I needed was you and it was nice to have the others."

They meandered to their car and chatted about all their dreams and some of the lovely things the parson had said. Then Johnny got a strange look on his face.

"So, now that we are married, will you tell me about

your silly plan to thwart Lawrence?"

"It's very humbling," she said.

"Good, maybe I can live up to you now."

So she told how she smacked her gum and played the extravagant actress and he would not stop laughing.

"You won't go and spend all my money, will you?" he asked in the middle of his laughing.

"I think I already have. Am I to be teased about this forever?"

"No, but it is so out of character for you, I can't help myself."

"I think we should go to dinner and you are not allowed to say a word of this to anyone!"

"I won't really, but I don't promise to not tease you once in a while. What a story. The poor guy. Did you ever tell him?"

"Not exactly, but I think he knew, at least a little. I am glad we became friends, it made up for my foolish ideas."

"What other strange secrets did I marry into?"

"I should have never told you." She sat pouting.

"Are you pouting or acting?"

"I am pouting for real!"

"Pouty Patty!" he said.

Then she started to laugh and he reached over and kissed her between giggles.

Epilogue

Thanksgiving 1906

"Has he come, yet?" Rose asked her for the third time.

"No, I'm afraid he won't be back in time," Margie said.

"We can't hold off too much longer," Rose said.

"I know. But we can't have Thanksgiving without him. It is our first Thanksgiving married and with Chipper as our son." Margie tried not to sound disappointed and sent Chipper and Coll out to watch.

Why was Johnny concerned about that silly envelope anyway? The message said to come to Rockfish Bay and see a man who said he had something from Johnny's uncle that had to do with the shipping business and it was important. Johnny had to go because David had gone to Doc's for Thanksgiving.

She heard honking and ran outside. But when she

got there, it wasn't Johnny but David, Doc, and Dahlia.

"Why you teases! You knew all along you were coming."

"Yes, but we didn't opt for car trouble. Did we miss dinner?" Dahlia said.

"No, but it is ready."

"I can't believe I will be sitting down for Thanksgiving dinner and not cooked any of it," Dahlia said.

"That is a good thing. We shall spoil you." Margie hugged her friend's arm and they walked down to Rose's.

"Where is Johnny?" Doc asked.

"He drove down the coast, Doc, but I want to ask you something," Chipper said, grabbing Doc's hand and pulling him down so he could whisper in his ear. "Can I call you grandpa?"

"I wouldn't have it any other way." Doc winked at Chipper, put his grandfatherly arm around the little boy's shoulder and the two walked proudly to Rose's.

The others watched and waited and followed them, as Margie elaborated the explanation. "Johnny has not come back from his errand down the coast. An envelope came saying the man wanted to see Johnny right away. I asked him if it could wait until after Thanksgiving but he said the man insisted and God was urging him to go. It had something to do with his uncle's shipping business," Margie said.

Rose insisted they couldn't wait any longer. They all sat and Margie started at every noise outside, hoping it was Johnny.

"I am sorry to be late!" Johnny came in grinning.

She knew that grin. He was up to something. "Oh, Johnny, you almost missed it and with the whole family here."

"I know but no one will mind when you hear what I have to tell you. But let's pray and eat."

As the group started eating, Johnny stood. "Ladies and gentlemen, I have unbelievably good news. My uncle left something in the hands of a man, a friend of his, who lives down the coast. He told the man before he died that if I reconstructed the shipping business and it starting running well, then he was to give this to me. It was from the sale of my uncle's properties. And what this means is that we can build our little town. Our homes on the bluff, Rose's cafe, and many other things eventually. But this is our start."

They sat in awe and when the shock wore off, they ate joyfully and discussed the kinds of things they would love to see in their town, which they decided should be called Majesty, to the glory of God.

Then, about the time for the pies to be served, Johnny stood up and looked among his friends and beloved new family and Margie noticed his eyes were wet with emotion.

"When I think back and see how the hand of God took us from our lonely, solitary states and brought us to be a family, and now even a town, I am blessed that he said that he sets the solitary in families, for now I know how true it is and I am so thankful." His heartwarming voice resonated in every heart and there was only one who wasn't sniffling, too young to understand anything but that he had been lovingly redeemed and now had a family once again. Chipper sat staring at his new father with a grin very reminiscent of Johnny's schoolboy grin.

Acknowledgments

With every book comes a multitude of precious people who work to make it the best it can possibly be. I would like to thank all the helpful editors and friends who fought to get me on target. You are a blessing.

Always, I am indebted to the prayer warriors, including family, friends and my Heart Wings sisters who kept me from falling apart at the seams when I fought many physical issues through the writing of this book.

Thank you dear Mindy Sato, at www.heartsongcalligraphy.com, for your beautiful scripture calligraphy in the front of my book. As always it blesses me.

A special thank you to my dear husband who survived the wild ride and never complained. You are my beloved.

A joyful thank you to my fabulous photographer kids, Matthew and Cheyenne Wilson, who captured my dear granddaughter, Annah, perfectly on the cover.

Thank you, Miss Annah, for being a lovely "Margie".

Did my book minister to you? If so, I would love to hear from you. Contact me through my website and click on the contact page or social media.

Sandy's website: www.sandyfayemauck.com

Facebook author page: Sandy Faye Mauck

Twitter @sandyfayemauck

Some Reviews For More Than She Dreamt

"More Than She Dreamt by Sandy Faye Mauck is a wonderful piece of fictional art." *Cheryl Baranski — CherylBBookBlog*

"I really cannot do this book justice! Sandy Faye Mauck has written a wonderful book that really touched my heart. More Than She Dreamt is a book that will stay with me for quite awhile. I HIGHLY recommend this book to anyone who enjoys Christian Historical Fiction, you will NOT be disappointed." *Beth Millinski — For the Love of Books*

"There are many good books in the world but this one is something extra special. It has the ability to really get into and speak to your heart. It is beautifully written and full of godly truths that will penetrate your soul." *Julia Wilson — Christian Bookaholic*

Book 1 in the *Rose Arbor Brides Series*

Book 2

<u>More Than She Imagined</u>

is coming soon!

Made in the USA
Las Vegas, NV
31 March 2023

69955475R00132